AMERICAN IN
TRANSLATION

AMERICAN IN TRANSLATION

A Novel in Three Novellas

Concha Alborg

To order additional copies of this book, contact:
Xlibris Corporation
1-888-795-4274
www.Xlibris.com
Orders@Xlibris.com
95833

Contents

MARINE CORPS WIFE

I

Paul left for Vietnam on an icy, gray February morning just a few weeks after our daughter was born. We had moved back to the Indiana College Town where we had met, and where our parents still lived, exactly fourteen days after the baby's arrival. We barely had time to find a furnished apartment, unpack the boxes, and buy a used car for me—my very first, as I had recently gotten my driver's license.

The night before his departure, Paul's parents gave him a good-bye party, inviting the immediate family and a few close friends. I didn't feel much like going since as far as I was concerned, there was nothing to celebrate. But the Davidsons, particularly Paul's mother, were so proud of their *Semper fi* first lieutenant going overseas to serve his country. I didn't want to rock the boat, as I had been known to do, with my unhappiness at the prospect of the year ahead, living alone with my firstborn child; so, of course, I went.

Looking now at the few photos we took, I appear sad and tired. My black hair is tied up in a stiff bun, and my dark eyes look darker than usual with big rings under them—not bad, though, for someone scared to death. Paul seems stunned, awkward in civilian clothes and a shaved head, his icy blue eyes open wide. It surprises me now to see how trim and young he looks, but it shouldn't, since he was only twenty-four years old then, three years older than I.

There is quite a contrast with the photos in the airport on the departure date, where he looks earnest, as if at attention. He's wearing his full uniform, the lieutenant bars gleaming from the camera's flash and his hat cocked just at the right angle; he hadn't made it through Officer Training School in record time for nothing. Laura is innocently sound asleep in the portable infant seat that her father holds rather stiffly. I try to imagine how I must have felt and discover that it's much harder than analyzing some old photos. I remember wanting the flight number to be called, to see the plane take off, to be back in the apartment, waking up the next day so that the clock could start ticking away the long minutes, days, weeks, months that lay ahead.

Then we were all surprised when the airplane started to turn around on the runway as Paul's father's name was called over the loudspeaker.

"Dr. Paul Davidson, Dr. Paul Davidson, please come to TWA's ticket counter."

The strangest thoughts crossed my mind: Perhaps my husband had come to his senses and we were moving to Canada after all. Maybe he had changed his mind and was going to enroll in a graduate program as I had begged him to do, or he was going to use the birth of our child as his rightful deferment from overseas duty. Perhaps, heaven forbid, he had a heart attack at such an early age like his maternal grandfather, who had died at twenty-nine, leaving two daughters and a young wife behind.

None of the above. Paul had left his military orders in the car. His father ran to the parking lot to retrieve the precious, irrevocable document. The rest of us didn't know whether to cry or laugh. My mother pronounced it a good omen: "Eso es buena suerte." In accordance with the Spanish tradition, if one forgets something, it means that he's coming back. After six years in the United States, my mother still didn't speak much English, particularly to express her old-country wisdom. For once, rather than feeling embarrassed by her ethnicity, I was hoping she was right. It was a good thing that my father had stayed home, or he would have been angry at her, as he often was. With his two PhDs, not only did he hate my mother's wisdom, but he had also fought—and lost—in the Spanish Civil War and now was a pacifist. The thought of anyone leaving for battle made his Latin temper rise, and here his son-in-law was going voluntarily, leaving a brand-new baby behind.

In retrospect, the decision to spend that year close to my parents doesn't seem very smart. I had forgotten how tense my parents were with each other since they had come back from Spain at the end of my dad's sabbatical the prior school year. I also had to contend with my father's pacifist attitude, which seemed un-American to my in-laws. Whatever my position about the war, a college campus in 1967 was a very unfriendly place for a Marine Corps wife. But I had already made this decision when my mother was diagnosed with a serious liver ailment.

And this turn of events, and the thought of sharing the first grandchild with her, confirmed that I was doing the right thing. In fact, during those years, service wives were not allowed (as they are nowadays) to live on the bases while their husbands were deployed. Nevertheless, many women used to stay in the area to serve as a support system for one another. I felt miscast in the role of a military dependent (as we were called), and I wanted to live in an environment I was familiar with, or so I thought.

However, few things were the same as before. My college friends were still on campus planning to graduate that spring, but I hadn't kept in touch with them after leaving to get married in the middle of my sophomore year. I wasn't going to show up among them now with a baby in tow and a husband in Vietnam while they were busy demonstrating against the war. A few days before he left, when we drove through the campus on a memory tour, Paul and I ran into some disorganized groups wearing flowers in their hair, carrying signs, chanting,

"Make *love*, not *war*. Make-*love*-not-*war*! Make *love*, not *war*. Make-*love*-not-*war*!"

"LBJ, how many babies did you kill today? L-B-J, how many babies did you kill todaaay?"

"Arms are for hugging. Arms are for huuugging!"

Paul had said in a dismissive tone, "What a bunch of assholes. What do they know? They're probably stoned."

Most of that year, I hid from my friends, avoiding any events at the university. I had come back as a dutiful daughter to be near my parents, and I felt lucky to find a first-floor apartment in the very same complex where they lived. I would be able to eat the two o'clock meal with them—they were still on a Spanish schedule—and they could fuss over and spoil their first grandchild to their hearts' content, also in Spanish style. My mother had hoped to remain behind in Madrid with my brother who, in her view, really needed her, unlike me who had left school early and had married too young. Now that I found myself in a fine predicament with a new baby and the husband gone, my mother felt needed after all.

"Ya tienes el zapatito de tu pie," another favorite saying in her repertoire, a form of Spanish poetic justice, so to speak: if the shoe fits . . .

Despite all my parents' rhetoric, the Davidsons were even harder to read, although I remember them taking their responsibilities in earnest, especially as Laura became a little older. Unfortunately, I wasn't such a dutiful daughter-in-law. Not so deep down, I blamed my gung ho in-laws for Paul's decision to join the marines. His father had been a colonel during World War II, had fought valiantly in Guadalcanal, and had come home a hero. His mother reminded me at every chance she had.

"Inmaculada, dear. You really are very lucky. You know that your husband is coming back in thirteen months. We had no idea when the war would be over. Little Paul was three years old before he saw his father."

Lucky, indeed! How could I have guessed when I met Paul that his parents—the sophisticated, Harvard-educated college professor and his Boston wife—were hawks in academic disguise? I tried not to see them too much, and since they lived a few miles away from the center of town in a rambling old country home, I had a built-in excuse; I was an inexperienced new driver.

And then there was baby Laura, like a ball to be tossed between the two sets of grandparents, not that everyone was ready and happy to be a grandparent. My father, for one, thought that he was much too young to be an *abuelito* as, according to him, he looked years younger than his age. He usually had some flirtation going on with one of his university students—those were the days before sexual harassment policies—and the last thing he wanted was a baby calling him grandpa in any language. My mother, on the other hand, transformed herself very easily into her new role of *abuelita*. She loved babysitting and making all kinds of outfits for the baby. Thank goodness she was there! As far as she was concerned, I had failed one more test by not knowing how to knit. What kind of mother could I possibly make? She was quick to remind me.

"Hasta para coser un botón, es mejor terminar la carrera primero." Whatever I did—even to sew on a button—would have been better if I finished my degree first. Now this was killing two birds with one stone!

On the eve of his departure, Paul and I had arrived from his good-bye party in a quiet mood. We both wanted to share some kind of tender moment before he left, but Laura was cranky and needed instant attention. When we finally got to bed, I felt like crying. My fears about the upcoming year were stronger than any sexual passion. Paul, on the other hand, was determined to make love.

"Please, Paul. You know we are not supposed to have intercourse. It hasn't been six weeks yet," I pleaded.

"Don't be silly, Inma, baby. You've been feeling great. Nothing is going to happen," he insisted, to no avail.

He sat on the side of the bed, frustrated with me. If he was feeling worried about leaving, he didn't say. It was as if everything depended on this one act of passion. He was aroused already, so I kept caressing him as steadily as I could. It didn't take him long to climax in my arms, on top of my belly, and fall fast asleep, as if all the anxiety had finally drained out of him. I lay there next to him for a long time before I could get to sleep, knowing full well how much I was going to miss him in the following months; missing him already.

II

———————

I had never seen a military base in my life until I arrived with Paul's parents in Quantico, Virginia, before our wedding. We stayed in guest quarters, thanks to the retired colonel's pedigree, but we didn't see Paul until the morning of his graduation from Officer Training School, the first of many honors he would receive. For me it was a stop before flying to Madrid, where we were getting married in a mere two weeks. We had chosen the day after Christmas, my parents' anniversary as well, for the big date. It was also the end of the semester; I would have to take the finals in January after a brief honeymoon in my hometown, the Spanish capital.

I brought a suitcase filled with my trousseau and some clothes I had bought in preparation for married life. In a bigger suitcase, I carried my wedding gown, which I had also bought myself, off the sale rack but in the fanciest store in town: one store, one stop, one trip, and voilà—the dress. Amazing how this bargain transformed itself in the announcement that my mother-in-law wrote for the *Boston Herald* and the local paper, the *Journal and Courier*: "The bride wore a bell-shaped bridal gown of white *peau de soie* with a bateau neckline and long sleeves tapering into bridal points, trimmed with corded alençon lace and featuring a cathedral train extending from the shoulders with a silk illusion veil and a coronet of illusion roses designed by Mrs. Juan José Abello." I still have the famous dress up in the attic somewhere, and I do find it beautiful to this day.

With all the excitement of the parade and the military protocol, we didn't recognize Paul right away. His mother was the first one to spot him.

"Paul, dear, you have changed so much in three months. You have lost weight."

Not only that, but he had also shed all his hair, and of course, he was wearing his complete winter dress uniform, which would become his own wedding gear. His loving mother would have described it this way, had she had a chance: "The groom was wearing a white wide-rimmed hat with the Marine Corps emblem on its brim, a navy blue belted jacket with rows of brass buttons, epaulets on the shoulders, and lieutenant bars on the high collar with charcoal gray trousers trimmed in red stripes." However, I was mortified at seeing his shaved head, knowing that it would be a source of mirth in Spain, where people shaved their hair only in case of a serious, debilitating illness such as typhoid fever. But he didn't look sick; in fact, he looked rather strong and determined, a new expression on his face.

"You look great, sweetheart," I told him, always saying what he wanted to hear.

The whole graduation day was spent in formal ceremonies, a lunch at the officers' club, and a reception that evening for select, distinguished guests such as ourselves. Paul and I weren't alone until the Davidsons left the following morning.

We spent the day touring the base in the used mint-green Rambler Paul had just bought. He showed me proudly the forbidding obstacle course, the barracks, the PX, the infirmary, and officers' housing, where we would be assigned a townhouse in a few weeks.

"How do you like it, baby?"

"It looks huge, almost a fenced-in city." I didn't want to say that it seemed like a prison.

It all felt strange to me in its neatness and quietness, as if it were a movie set. Like it or not, this place was going to be our first home, and I was anxious and curious at the same time. I was fast becoming an expert in transformation—from a Spanish schoolgirl to a college coed in the States, from an independent young woman to a military wife. I remember smelling the pine trees all around the compound and thinking how that Virginia scent was reminiscent of the trees in the Retiro Park, back in Madrid, although even the pinecones were different and much bigger here. Just as strange was getting reacquainted again.

"I missed you terribly during the last three months, sweetheart," I said, trying to change the subject to something more romantic.

"Me too, but it's over now. Soon we'll be together every day," he assured me.

I wish we had known then that the discipline of Officer Training School—which forbade visits, restricted phone calls, and allowed limited time for letter writing—would be very good training for his later duty in Vietnam. The overwhelming feeling of loneliness was the major factor behind our decision to move up the wedding date. It wasn't that I was pregnant, as my father suspected when we told my parents. In fact, I was still a virgin. Not that we hadn't made out like crazy in the little MG Paul had during college or, on special occasions, if we were lucky, in his father's Oldsmobile, where I lost a demure pearl necklace. But "going all the way"—as it was called then—was out of the question. More than once we found ourselves peeling our clothes off, rolling in the backseat, saved by the shining lights of an oncoming car or the flashlight of a policeman patrolling the local lovers' lane. One of our most daring escapades—aside from skipping class to see the Beatles at the Indiana State Fair—consisted of skinny-dipping in a college friend's pond, and I say this not because we were naked, but because there was lightning and thundering right on top of us during a typical Midwestern summer thunderstorm.

That last weekend together before our wedding—when Paul's parents left after his OTS graduation and we checked into a motel right outside the base—was, in a way, the beginning of our honeymoon.

"I've started the birth-control pills, you know?" I reminded Paul as soon as we were alone. "Then we don't need to wait any longer. What difference does it make now?" Paul said.

"I thought we agreed to wait until our wedding night in Madrid. What could be more romantic than that?" I've always been an expert in giving mixed signals.

One of my parents' friends, who worked as a chef at the Ritz Hotel, had given us three nights in the honeymoon suite as a present. Now that was something worth waiting for! We did sleep together in the motel—in the literal sense of the word only—naked, despite all the sexy nightgowns in my trousseau, and much more comfortably than in the old MG. We both were exhausted after hours of the sheer pleasure of hugging each other, rolling on the bed, caressing our young bodies, feeling our tongues touching and exploring as we hadn't done before, getting farther from the Old World Catholic dating we had been used to. At one point during the night, we heard a distant police siren, and we jumped momentarily, as if we were still in a car, doing something forbidden. We were very much in love then, anticipating years of happiness together.

III

————————

Before Paul's first letter arrived from Vietnam, he called from Okinawa, but I was so alarmed just to hear the phone ring late at night, and there was such an echo to our connection that we could hardly hear each other. I had to scream and feared I'd wake up the baby, just when I was trying to get her to sleep through the night.

"How come you are calling so late, sweetheart? Is anything wrong?"

"Don't forget that we are thirteen hours ahead of you," he reminded me. "I just got notified that I've been promoted to captain.

"How was your sixth-week checkup? Did you like the doctor? Are you feeling well?" He surprised me by asking since he had been so withdrawn the last few days before he left.

"Fine, everything is fine. I'll wait a couple of months and I'll start the pill again."

"Why so soon?" He seemed puzzled.

"I want to be ready when we meet for R&R." I felt hurt that he wasn't already thinking about it, as I was.

"Baby, we haven't even left Japan!"

————

He sounded disappointed not to be in Vietnam yet. It was all very confusing to me, although perhaps it shouldn't have been. He had been training to go to war ever since he joined the Marine Corps more than two years earlier, and he was eager to be where the action was. His squadron had left for Japan earlier while he waited behind for the baby to be born and to move us back home. But I was still hurt. Of course, I said nothing of it.

"I'm very proud of you, sweetheart. I'm really happy about your promotion," I tried to sound encouraging.

I was also jealous of the other wives who had gone to Okinawa with their men for a few weeks before deployment to Vietnam, something which—being nine months pregnant—I hadn't been able to do. I cried, frustrated, when we hung up, feeling guilty for not being more supportive and not knowing if or when he'd be able to call again.

I know I must sound like my mother-in-law when she compared her war with mine, but I can't help thinking that at least communication is so much easier nowadays for military families with cell phones and e-mail. I guess everyone thinks their own war is the hardest. It's also true that we didn't have any kind of help or instruction about what to expect while our spouses were overseas, even though many of us were so young. The only advice I remember hearing came from a general in North Carolina: "Be thankful that your husbands are aviators. They can't come back with missing limbs, crippled or hurt as infantrymen often do. They'll come back either with their dog tags between their teeth as identification [quite a fine prospect that was!] or all in one piece, as a good marine should." He mentioned nothing of the possibilities of being held as a prisoner of war, and we hadn't heard yet of post-traumatic stress disorder or any of the psychological terminology now associated with war.

Early that year, I had decided that I wouldn't watch the television news or read the local newspapers. I didn't want to hear how many American planes had been shot down that day or see the carnage on the TV screen. I kept only the subscription to *Time*, which at least identified the type of plane and the service branch. As long as it wasn't a marine F-4 Phantom, I felt safe. Besides, by the time the news was reported in the magazine, I would have been notified if something awful had already happened. It still bothered me to read about all the demonstrations against the war and the editorials for an end to the conflict. I felt as if I were in hiding because my husband was in Vietnam, and I found myself defending him in front of my parents and their academic friends, although I didn't believe in the war myself. A typical afternoon conversation could easily turn into a confrontation.

"Paul always says that it's his duty to serve, that it's a matter of principle," I'd say, knowing that my parents didn't agree.

"Y tú, qué piensas tú." My mother, never one to keep anything in, would press me for my opinion. She always knew how to push my buttons.

"I'm just worried about my husband, *Mamá*, in case you haven't noticed."

In the meantime, my mother-in-law truly felt that her son was a hero. She kept every newspaper article that reported anything about his base in Chu Lai: the

Silver Eagles, his squadron; Major Thomas Duffy, his commanding officer; and F-4 Phantoms. Of course, she bombarded the alumni magazine, the local papers, and the *Boston Herald* with the latest details, embellishing with the same gusto with which she had written about my wedding dress. After all, her name wasn't Constance for nothing.

Only years later did I discover two huge bulging albums that my mother-in-law put together, some sort of military journal or war chronicle, and I don't know whether to be thankful that she kept such extraordinary records—a great trove for my writing—or be mad that she wrote her own hawkish version of the war and her son's contribution to it. In moments of despair, I even blamed his mother for Paul's decision to be a marine. I am now certain that, seeking her second chance at patriotic fame, it was she who was behind Paul's career. No wonder she never told me about the albums! I must have been such a disappointment to her with my critical attitude and constant questioning of the war. Unbeknownst to me then, the two of us really were antagonists, replaying some absurd version of the Spanish-American War. There she was, saving every bit of news I didn't even want to see. I can still hear her words.

"Inmaculada, dear, you should be proud of your husband," she liked to remind me. "He's a real hero."

Only to be followed by my snappy answer,

"Connie, don't forget that I didn't volunteer for this tour of duty. I was drafted, okay?" Another relative who had a way to get the worst out of me.

IV

I had no real friends my own age, except for an occasional contact with other mothers with babies in the apartment complex. I concentrated most of my energies on taking care of Laura, and yes, I did make a precious album of the baby's first year that I planned to give her father when he returned from Vietnam. Sewing was something else I enjoyed. When I was a young girl in Madrid, we had to take sewing in school. During the last year—I guess in preparation for the real world—we made a baby's layette. I have to confess that it was my favorite sewing project. I made it out of blue muslin and it fit Manolín, my baby-boy doll, perfectly. No wonder I loved taking care of Laura, although deep down inside I had thought that I would be a writer first and a mother much later. I didn't venture making dresses for her or anything too complicated since we were so modern in America, but I did make receiving blankets, bibs, and sheets for the bassinet with matching curtains; and I even painted a rocking chair and a chest of drawers for her room—the only furniture we weren't renting—which Paul and I ordered unfinished from the Sears catalogue.

My first obsession was to get Laura to sleep through the night. Since I was on my own with her, there were no turns to be taken feeding or watching her. Some mornings I'd get up to find two or three bottles in the kitchen, although I couldn't remember having been up even once. Taking a shower or washing our clothes in the laundry room at the end of the hall were additional challenges; anything I needed to do had to be coordinated with her naps. After having lived in the South for a couple of years, the Midwestern winter seemed endless. As an inexperienced new driver, I particularly hated driving in the snow, but I somehow managed to keep all the doctor's appointments for the baby and even took my mother to hers whenever I could.

Soon Laura and I had our own little routine; from the very first days of early spring, I took her for walks in an English buggy we had bought at the base, used but in excellent condition. I wrote to Paul religiously, and if there was any time left, I read the current selection of the Book-of the-Month-Club, the only concession to my intellectual life in those days. I remember reading Truman Capote's *In Cold Blood*, not a very good selection for someone living alone, and *The Confessions of Nat Turner*, which made a big impression on me, after my own Southern experiences. I had witnessed racism with alarm, including in the military, where I hadn't seen a single black officer.

Almost every day we spent a few hours at the *abuelitos'* place. Usually, I ate a big lunch with them. For the first time in my life, I took an interest in my mother's recipes and helped her in the kitchen, learning to make paella, gazpacho, flan. Paul would like that, I thought, since I knew that the more stereotypically Spanish I was, the better. In fact, I was not the prototype of the hot-blooded Spaniard any more than he was a cool-headed Anglo. He had this *Spanishization* in common with my parents, who saw his tour of duty as another chance to steer me in the right direction. They succeeded, for example, in having Laura's ears pierced, something that wasn't done to little American girls in those days. My Spanish relatives had sent some jewelry as baby gifts, and it seemed to matter a lot to my parents. She did look cute with tiny coral or turquoise studs. There was no mistaking then that she was a little girl, despite her bald head. My father used to say about her,

"Se parece a los Davidsons," because he always blamed the in-laws for any of the baby's less-than-perfect traits.

I remember that the pacifier, which they had at the ready as soon as Laura uttered a peep, was a source of conflict.

"Dr. Spock advises against it—it's bad for the baby's teeth," I tried to explain to them.

"But she doesn't have any yet." My mother was always quick with her Old World logic. Sometimes I would rebel, just on principle: "I am her mother, and I know what is best for my baby!"

They also wanted to make sure that we spoke only Spanish to the baby. Heaven forbid she end up speaking Spanish with an American accent, as if they themselves didn't have a thick one when they spoke English.

"But she doesn't say a word yet." I was a quick learner myself.

Despite his early ambivalence at becoming a grandfather, my dad warmed up quickly to the idea. After our meal, he'd play with Laura for a long time instead of taking a nap as he was used to doing. When she started to crawl, the two of them would "chase" each other around the dining room table until my mother screamed in desperation that they were driving her crazy.

"¡Por Dios, Juanjo, que me vuelves loca!"

I don't think that we spoke a lot about the war or how I was feeling. They always wanted to know if I had a letter from Paul, but that was about it. The baby and how to bring her up properly consumed most of our conversations. I knew that when I wasn't around, they often argued about my brother living alone in Madrid and how much money he was spending. I could hear their voices as Laura and I arrived, but they'd change the subject when I was present.

The other topic of conversation was my mother's illness, although, in the Spanish tradition, we weren't honest about that either, as if she actually didn't know what was going on with her. We tried to focus on the practical aspects such as her diet, appointments, and medicines. For such a loud family, there were a lot of unspoken secrets. But despite the tensions, those few hours with my parents were my favorite part of the day. They helped the time go fast and made me appreciate when I found myself alone with the baby in the apartment. Laura, exhausted from the cultural clashes, usually slept the rest of the afternoon, giving me time for reading and my letter writing to Paul.

V

2200 23 March 1967

My dear Inma,

I was so happy to have your letters waiting for me when we arrived in Vietnam. And I loved the baby's pictures, it looks like she has grown a lot already. I'm glad to see that you are using the Polaroid camera.

Here I am in the oven of the earth, Chu Lai, Vietnam. The temperature has been 90-105 every day. However, surprisingly, I am getting quite used to it now. I have had a working party out for two or three days, and I can only make them work about twenty minutes, then we have to drink water and rest for ten. The first day I worked with them, now I put my pith helmet on and direct. We are moving some tropical huts and wrecking others.

Have been flying at least once a day. We fly anytime. I have been up sometimes at four o'clock in the morning. It's cool then.

Everyone is here from our old CO and from 531 to Group S-4. Remember Jim Jacobsen, Bob Henricksen, Mike Halpin, and George Rodosky? We have an O'Club, cold beer and everyone eats in an open mess. Food is fair, lots of beans, etc. My big gripe is the mail is not regular. It only comes in bunches when there is space available in the supply planes. Some men have already written their congressmen. But marines are tough, they don't need mail every day. But keep your letters coming, they make my day. I read them over and over until I think I have them memorized.

We live six people to a hut. When we were in Japan, we bought a washing machine and everyone does their own laundry. We also got a refrig from air force salvage in Tokyo, so we are not so bad off.

Flying is very exciting as you might guess, especially when you are in support of ground troops. The other day, my first hop, we hit a fortified VC village, which had an automatic weapon. We destroyed the gun, then knapped the village while a helicopter came in to get a recon team out, which had been pinned down by the automatic weapon.

I have already lost track of the days of the week and have to backtrack to figure which day it is. That's the way I like it.

The only way to go to sleep is thinking about you in my arms. I just want to be home and start making a life with you and the baby.

All my love,
Paul

2145 13 April 1967

Dear wifey,

I keep waking up thinking about you, if you know what I mean. We are so busy during the day that there is no time to get horny. At night I crawl on my hands and knees to the rack. As you know, we work seven days a week.

Not much is really new. Same every day: get up, fly, sweat some, eat, a few beers in the evening, and sleep. Most everyone stays around the hut unless something pressing has to be done in the hangar area. Got used to the artillery flares and sporadic firefights the first week.

A catastrophic thing has happened, RIOs are being taken for FAC. I joined aviation to keep out of foxholes. Have twenty-plus missions, one and a half air medals, and have been "in country" twenty-three days, of which the first four I did not fly. Will have one hundred missions inside of three months easily. Did I tell you that a flight I was on has been put up for a DFC (distinguished flying cross), but the RIOs will probably be downgraded to a single strike air medal. Oh well, life is tough.

You sounded sad in a couple of your letters. Don't let my mother's comments get to you, and ditto with your father's wisecracks. If I were there, they wouldn't say those things. Then again, if I were there, we would be having our ashes hauled.

Your loving hubby,
Paul

2300 30 April 1967

Dear Inma,

Thanks for the pictures, the baby is looking real cute. Why don't you take some sexy ones of yourself with the Polaroid? I should have done that before I left. I guess I wasn't thinking then how much I was going to miss you.

Do you remember Hugh Fanning? His wife, Sylvia, took driving lessons with you. Well, they had another baby girl! We better have a boy next time, huh? I'm glad I stayed behind to at least see our baby some. It sounds like the two of you are having some fun. I agree with your parents, make sure she learns Spanish.

I am fairly well acclimatized, although I cant seem to stop sweating. Really havent lost much weight. Wasnt quite as scared as I thought I would be. However, coming out of the S-2 briefings, one wonders whether you have a snowballs chance in hell. It usually sounds like this, "Along your route of flight, you have automatic weapons, 37s, 57s small arms, and the fire has been heavy. They have the SAM radar on today and we expect them to fire between 1400 to 1600. You will be in the area at 1500, etc . . . . etc." Havent seen any fire, although have been fired on a number of times. You can almost feel it when they are firing. We went in on a target the other day where the Cong had shot down a UH-46, a UH-1E (two different types of helis), and an A-1. The crews were in a bomb crater, and the Cong were on a cliff above the whole deal. We dropped nape and 250s and received fire as we pulled out over the top of the cliff. We didn't see it, but the aircraft following us did.

I am the operations duty officer tonight, which entails staying up and keeping track of airplanes.

You cant say that I didnt write a lot today and with my feelings, etc . . . . hope there wasn't too much technical lingo. It's hard to think of anything else.

You are my love forever,
Paul

Look for a surprise on Mother's Day!

VI

Before Paul left for Vietnam, I suppose that base housing had been somewhat like living on a college campus, but playing dress-up soldiers and wives at the same time. Never mind that I hadn't finished my degree; a lot of the other women hadn't either. The men were out all day in some kind of training exercises or on preparations for deployment. The women hardly ever left the base. Although I don't even drink coffee, we met for informal *kaffeeklatsches* two or three times a week. Often, a captain's or a major's wife would come by to meet us, the new wives in town.

"I do declare if so many of you are not pregnant already! Y'all can't complain about the young marine lieutenants now, can *ya*?" I can still hear their Southern accent.

We had fancy luncheons at the officers' club to raise money for some cause or for an occasional fashion show. We all wore tailored suits with matching hats and white gloves. The best-dressed one was always Kissy Dupree; not only was she from the South, but also from a very genteel upbringing.

"Y'all like it, do *ya*? And here I didn't know what to *wiire*."

I can see these images now. We looked like children wearing our mother's clothes, except my mother never had anything that elaborate. There were all kinds of more formal events, special graduations, parades commemorating some important date, and weddings of young officers wearing their formal dress uniforms, who had waited a few more months than the rest of us to get married.

There was a couple down the street, the DiChiaras, who had married the exact same day as we had, and we became fast friends. Sue was already expecting—twins as it turned out. Our husbands rode to the barracks together in our car, and we kept Sue's car for errands and appointments. A perfect arrangement, considering that I didn't know how to drive yet. We even watched *Peyton Place* together, the hot TV program with Ryan O'Neal. Sue had a gorgeous wedding album with a million colored pictures of every second of the ceremony, row after row of matching attendants, and all her relatives smiling stiffly as if they were royalty (imagine what my mother-in-law would have done with all that raw material!).

"*Inmaaa*, now I can't believe that you only have these few black-and-white pictures of your wedding. You should at least put them in an album," Sue used to say since I kept them in a stationery box. In my wedding pictures, the relatives look elegant and serious, a bit like immigrants. I'm the only one smiling—contaminated already, I guess, by the happy Americans. Sue and I kept in touch for some time after they left the service, exchanging Christmas cards and pictures of family members in corny coordinated outfits. I wonder what became of the DiChiaras. A few years ago on a trip to Washington, I looked for his name at the Vietnam Veterans Memorial and was relieved that it wasn't on the Wall.

We moved so often that friendships were formed and lost in a hurry; there was no time to waste. During flight school, Adelle and Jim were our friends, though we really had nothing in common. If we hadn't met in the service, we would never have crossed paths. Adelle was game for anything. She wore flashy clothes, and her hair was platinum blond. She was what would later be called a Valley Girl from California.

"You gals are like Betty and Veronica," her husband used to say, but I wasn't familiar with that comic strip. Jim and Adelle were into fancy cars and already knew that they didn't want children. Of all the couples we met, they were the first to separate and eventually divorce after Jim's tour of duty in Vietnam.

There was no time to get bored either. No sooner had I made some friends at one base and gotten to know my way around, we had to move to another place. From Quantico we went to Pensacola for flight school, then to Georgia, back to Jacksonville, Florida, and then to North Carolina, where Laura was born—all this in just under two years. I think it mattered less to me than to most of the other wives. I was already far away from my homeland. One state turned out to be the same as another; it all was a foreign country in more ways than one. I didn't even send pictures to my relatives in Spain for fear they wouldn't understand why people move so often in the States and would think that I had lost my mind. My parents did visit us in North Carolina when I was already pregnant with Laura, and they were a model of restraint, fearful, I am sure now, of the Vietnam deployment hanging over our heads.

VII

Holidays and special occasions were the most trying times during that long year of separation. Paul sent roses for Mother's Day and that was fine, but it wasn't what I really wanted, which was to have my husband safe at home.

"Inmaculada, dear, aren't they just marvelous?" My mother-in-law acted surprised, although I knew she had ordered the flowers for her son.

"No te quejarás hoy también," My mother warned me not to complain for just one day.

I couldn't say that I would rather not have flowers around to remind me that my husband wasn't there. I was caught in a web of emotions I couldn't explain. I was in part a daughter, in part a mother, and in part a wife; but I didn't feel completely comfortable in any of those roles. I thought I had left my parents' home for good several years ago, but there I was, eating my meals with them again and listening to their bickering. Motherhood felt so new, almost like being in a play, and what kind of a family were we without the father and husband around? Even my name was strange to me, Mrs. Paul Davidson

Jr. Who the hell was that? I wish I had stuck to my guns and told everyone that in Spain women don't change their names when they marry, that I liked my name just as it was, Inmaculada Abello, which my own husband and our marine friends had shortened to a foreign-sounding "Inma." It wasn't unusual for me to end one of these existential crises arguing and exasperated with my mother, who constantly reminded me,

"You shouldn't have married so young."

"¡Ay, *Mamá*, por Dios! For god's sake, don't I have enough worries already?"

Then I would feel guilty for even worrying about these things when I knew I had other more important problems to think about. So much for Mother's Day!

With summer fast approaching, my mother started planning her yearly sojourn to Spain to see my brother, who unlike me (even though he was older) was in no hurry to get married. To my surprise, my father seemed happy to stay behind this time since I was there to cook his meals, or so he said. Talking about being caught in between two roles! *Abuelito* was not exactly the person I was thinking of when I learned some Spanish recipes. I remember that he constantly complained about everything I made.

"Necesita un poquito de sal." As if he couldn't use the saltshaker by himself.

The other prospect was to spend some vacation time in Maine with the American set of grandparents, which also didn't appeal to me, no matter how attractive their summer place could be. The baby was barely six months old, and it meant a long trip by car. When the dates for my mother's trip didn't work out well anyway, I decided to skip the trip to Maine. This confirmed to everyone that I was an oddball, as my mother had been saying all along.

"!Ay, hija, qué rara eres!"

A day that I'm sure I ruined for everyone was my brother-in-law's college graduation. Michael and I are close in age and used to run around with the same group of friends. In fact, it was he who introduced me to Paul during a hootenanny at the university featuring the popular trio Peter, Paul, and Mary. To see him graduate with my former classmates was the last thing I wanted to do. I felt bad because Paul Senior had been appointed dean of the business school by then, and graduation was an important event. I simply couldn't do it. I could handle the routine and my responsibilities, but the parties and the celebrations were just too painful to bear. They made me feel Paul's absence the way they say a person can still feel the pain after losing a limb. As it turned out, there was a big demonstration against the war in the midst of the ceremony; and at least my parents, if not Paul's, agreed with me that it was better I had stayed home.

Unlike his older brother, Michael had decided to join the National Guard to stay away from Vietnam. Amazingly, his parents thought nothing this time of using their influence to ensure him a cushy assignment. As far as I was concerned, life just wasn't fair. Not that I wished I had married the younger brother, since I really didn't care for him, and even less so during the ensuing year.

VIII

2200 15 May 1967

My dear wife,

I'm so glad you liked the roses for Mother's Day. I wish I could have been there with you. Next year we'll make up for each and every holiday. You'll see.

Things are not getting any easier here either. We don't have anything in Chu Lai. The PX only has toothpaste, soap, etc . . . . There is an O'Club that is not too bad. The ones that really get to me are the army grunts that come off the line. You see them coming in, bearded and all covered with dust, to buy dolls and jewelry to send home.

I went out to the dump the other day with a working party in my flight suit. We pulled up beside an army truck that had Vietnamese laborers. As soon as they saw me, they started to jabber and point to me. I got a little scared, so I pulled out my revolver and loaded it, just in case. All the enlisted men are being issued M16s. I hope to hell they know what they are doing when it's time to fire them.

Tell me more stories about the baby, I like to hear them. Does she really kiss my picture? She looks cute with those damn earrings.

When is she going to get any hair? Well, at least she looks like her old man.

I had another dream about you and me getting it on, with your long legs wrapped around me. I have never been so horny in my life,

Paul

2300 23 May 1967

Dear Inma,

What's this I hear about Michael's graduation? I know it's hard for you, but you could try going for his sake. Some people have all the luck, I grant you that.

The days are getting hotter, over one hundred degrees. At least during the night, there is usually a breeze and the temperature drops to the low eighties. You actually dont notice the heat unless you are exerting yourself, which I try not to do, at least not between nine in the morning and three in the afternoon.

Still flying about once a day, mostly in the DMZ and around Khe Sanh. I am sure you have read about those two places. I dont think you have read about the beating I am pretty sure the marines took in that area. Of course, no one tells us that kind of news either. However, I believe we did get whipped. There are seventy-five thousand marines in the I Corps area to control a population of over two million people. To meet the growing North Vietnamese threat in the western sectors and in the mountains, the marines have had to leave the coastal areas virtually undefended. You dont have to be a strategist to figure out what happens then.

What shitty mail service we get here at Chu Lai. As far as I can determine, the mail gets to Da Nang okay, but then it gets from there to here via space available on air force planes. It has to be a certain type of aircraft certified to carry mail, etc . . . . Consequently, we only get mail every three to four days. Tell my dad to speak to Senator Bayh or anyone else he sees.

What's new in Indiana? The Indianapolis Star sends me a weekly summary of the sports, but since I am not an avid sports fan, cant say I devour them. Nice effort on their part, though.

I guess I don't sound too cheerful myself today. I am closing this letter and going to sleep to dream about you. Best part of my day anyway. All my love to you and little Laura,

Paul

2130 5 June 1967

Dear sweetheart,

Finally have some exciting news! It looks like I will be going to the Philippines for Jungle Survival. I wanted to go to Japan for Sea Survival as I have been to Jungle Survival in Panama, remember? I guess I don't get my way. They give you about a week to attend to military matters for each school day. Decent. Wish you could come, of course. I will look for some things to buy for the apartment.

It sounds as if you are getting around more with the baby. I am sure that having spring weather helps. Havent heard of the movies you mention. There is absolutely no diversion here. The movie (outdoor) is so terrible I hardly ever go, you know I don't like them as much as you do. One good thing is that it is extremely easy for the days to run together, and before you know it, all track of time is lost and the weeks go by.

Whatever happened to the Polaroid shots you were going to take of yourself? I don't know if I can wait for R&R. At least ask your dad to take some with the new bathing suit.

I will keep you posted about the trip to the Philippines. Keep writing your letters, though. Hopefully, I will have a bunch waiting for me when I get back.

Your adoring husband,
Paul

IX

Thank goodness for the baby. She was growing so fast and learning new things every day, it was impossible not to feel joy just watching her. I remember the first morning she woke up after I did. I ran into her room thinking that something had happened to her. In fact, I woke her and she looked up from her crib and gave me this big smile. From then on, many mornings I would lie in bed quietly, waiting for her to stir. She used to make the sweetest sounds. I talked with her nonstop all day.

"Good morning, sunshine. How did we sleep last night, huh?" And she'd smile and coo back as if she knew what I was saying. After breakfast, I'd give her a bath, usually on top of her dressing table, which was much easier than in the large bathtub.

"My, you are getting *sooo* big. You won't be quite as tall as your daddy, will you?"

She was growing out of her clothes quickly. For the first months, she could still wear many of the outfits we got as baby gifts, but I knew I would have to start sewing soon to stay on my budget. There wasn't a PX anywhere nearby. Not that I missed it, other than the good prices for brand names.

Grandfather Davidson was good about coming over and visiting us during Laura's lunchtime. I liked seeing him. Paul looked so much like his dad already. Looking at his father helped me imagine how Paul would mature into a solid-looking man with square features and bright blue eyes. Grandpa often brought the video camera and would follow us around, whatever we were doing, and shoot some film.

"Are you ladies beautiful enough for a documentary?" His phone call would alert us that company was on its way.

"Let's hurry up, baby doll, a very important person is coming—your Yankee grandpa."

There she'd be sitting in the infant seat, eating her favorites—plums and peaches—or holding her own bottle and kicking her legs rhythmically. Soon she needed a high chair and was staying awake most of the morning, entertaining herself in the playpen.

We saw less of Grandma, who was always busy doing errands around town, seeing people, and keeping up with her gazetteer duties. She also played tennis with her friends regularly. She had an athletic build with strong, heavy legs, such a contrast to my mother who looked weaker all the time. During that year, my mother-in-law decided to take some Russian courses at the university. Her own mother—*Mère*, in honor of the French side of the family—was still alive then, and she took care of the cooking and practically ran the house. She made a daily shopping list for Constance, who would run into the supermarket at the last possible moment of the day and fly home down the river road at rush hour.

Our paths didn't cross very often, as we certainly ran in different circles, especially since Paul Senior had been appointed dean and they had so much entertaining to do. Until I saw the Vietnam albums, I had forgotten they had gone to Chile and Argentina and to South Africa on some school-recruiting trips that year. Not surprisingly, Laura recognized the Spanish grandparents a lot sooner than their American counterparts, and I am sure there were all kinds of competition going on among them.

The couple of months my mother stayed in Spain seemed eternal. Not only did my father complain about my cooking, but he was also moodier than usual, simply bad company. I missed my mother, and not just because she wasn't there to cook. Despite all her critical comments, my mother was my sounding board, the only person I could vent my feelings to without fear. My father had bought a red Mercury Cougar for himself and took long drives in the afternoon to a nearby lake or who knew where else. I suspected that he was involved with some student again, but mostly I stayed out of his way. I really didn't understand how my mother put up with him.

The apartment pool had opened, and many afternoons I sat there reading while the baby slept in the stroller since she had outgrown her English buggy. I had no idea how Spanish babies stayed in theirs until they were one year old or more. Laura was definitely an American and would continue to be. I would make sure of that.

"And let's hope you don't have a funny accent like your momma, yes?"

I still looked very Spanish myself, with my long hair in a formal bun on top of my head and a modest bikini that I had worn before the pregnancy. The young people around me were a lot more casual in their hippy getups. Men and women alike wore their hair long, down and unkempt, and their bathing suits were much skimpier than mine. Maybe my mother was right about my being an odd duck. Where in the world did I fit in? Worst of all, I was sure that I would feel equally out of place if I suddenly appeared in Madrid at our old swim club with a baby in my arms.

I kept in touch with a couple of the other military wives, who confessed to having similar problems fitting in. Adelle was back in California, living alone and taking courses at UCLA as if she had never been married.

"Listen, Inma," she told me during our last phone call, "R&R was a big disappointment. Jim was only interested in having sex. Forget about sightseeing or even lying on the beach."

Paul and I were starting to plan our trip, and I hadn't decided whether to take Laura.

"Are you crazy?" Adelle said. "Remember Sue DiChiara? She took the twins with her and regretted it. The long flights to and from Hawaii were unbearable." But in any case, Adelle didn't know what it was like to have a baby.

One thing I was sure of, judging from what I saw at the pool—I had to get a new bathing suit, a sexy little number. Paul would like that. I kept fantasizing about being with my husband on R&R. I could close my eyes and see myself in the sun on a beautiful beach in Hawaii. I had never been there, but it was more real than the pool where I actually was. We would be swimming underwater, hugging each other, and Paul would be touching my breasts with their hard nipples showing through the bathing suit. We used to laugh that his dick—as he called it—would shrink underwater, but not in Hawaii, I thought, where it would be so warm. I could feel him, hard against my thighs, until Laura's whimpering brought me back to reality.

X

2345 25 June 1967

My dear Inma,

Sorry to hear that you won't be going to Maine this year. I can imagine that it would be difficult with the baby and all, but I know that my parents would have loved it, if nothing else, to show Laura off to all their friends.

I called twice from the Philippines, but you werent home. So frustrating. I could tell that the connection wasnt good anyway. I had the operator try it to no avail. Oh well.

Enjoyed myself there, I liked it better than Japan for some things. I saw some beautiful wood things, they seem to be good craftsmen. They have a nice-looking wood called monkeypod. I bought a lazy Susan, a salad bowl set, and a surprise decoration for the apartment. Hope you like them.

I did see the miniskirts you mentioned, very attractive! I can just imagine how sexy you would look with your long legs. The beaches are beautiful there. Just took a quick tour to see everything.

Thanks for the pipe tobacco you sent (I didn't have any) and the other goodies. It was all waiting for me when I got back.

I will write very soon. Need to catch some zs now. I love you,

Paul

1540 4 July 1967

Dear Inma,

I was just awarded my first air medal. Have earned five, got my second (a gold star) before I got the first. Bet you are going to be very proud of your hubby.

I am now one of three group intelligence briefing officers. I debrief the flights one day, I brief the next, and then have a day off. During my day off, I have to fly three times to keep up an average of one/day. Makes time pass fast, weeks go by at the turn of your head—amazing.

Just finished reading the newspaper and saw where Johnson is asking for a 10 percent tax increase to offset a possible 23 billion federal deficit. Everyone I talk with and see daily is fed up with him. One man from Texas says he cant see in Johnson any other image but that of a county sheriff in the rural South. Wish, wish, wish the president would get the job done here. I feel the communists are in a stronger position militarily and most likely politically, now more than ever before. We get whipped every time we turn around. They hit and run, hit and run, and we cant cope with that. Lots of trouble in the Middle East too, I see. Never cared much for Israel, you know that.

Wonder what you are doing this holiday. Sitting at the pool, I bet. Wish I could be a fly on the wall. Better yet, be the lifeguard who rescues you in my arms. Hope you are not too lonely without your mom and my parents (ha, ha). Sorry that your dad is not very good company. He's only nice/funny when he wants to be.

Lots of hugs and wet kisses,
Paul

2300 17 July 1967

My dear Inma,

Good pictures of you with the bikini and the minidress. It looks like you have a tan. I knew you wouldnt use the Polaroid. Don't worry, I'm not showing any pictures to anybody.

Some of the men have been going to R&R already, and they say that coming back is the hardest thing they ever did. Seems that Jim and Adelle had a great time. I'll put in for late October, close to your birthday and over half time. Sounds good? Hope your mother feels up to babysitting. Really want to see the baby, but it isn't as if she knows me or anything.

Am getting used to the heat in Nam now. 106, which is about the temperature we have every day, doesnt seem bad at all, 85 degrees seems cool. Bought a fan in the Philippines so I can sleep well. Actually, nights are cool anyway. A couple of nights have had to put my poncho over to keep warm.

I was down to 195 lbs. but put five on in the Philippines. Usually only eat once or twice a day, plus am never hungry. Have to force myself to eat. The food is good—some air force pilots who had trouble with their aircraft stopped here and said they were coming here once a week to eat as their food is so bad.

I wrote to my dad telling him that General Greene is coming on August 10, and we have to put a show on for him—I find it hard to believe we are actually going to tie up four aircraft for approx half a day for a show for him. The stuff they are going to show him we never do anyway—it just looks good (the SATS strip). They ought not let any generals or politicians come here—only field commanders.

We had to fly cover for McNamara.

What's this you tell me about your dad's new car? Don't even think about taking it for a ride. Cant imagine he'd let you anyway. We'll rent a car in Hawaii and do some driving around the island, I promise. We'll do a lot more than that, just you wait. I cant wait to have you naked in my arms and roll in bed with you. How does that sound to you?

Love you a bunch,
Paul

XI

As soon as my mother was back from Spain, we had an ugly argument that upset me for a long time. My father went to pick her up in Chicago, and I could tell she was in a bad mood the minute I saw her. She probably disapproved of the new sports car, or maybe she felt jet-lagged. Laura and I were anxiously waiting for her at the apartment. She came loaded with gifts for the baby from relatives and friends, and she also bought her a white furry winter coat, trimmed in pink with a matching hat for the upcoming winter.

"Es bonito, pero no muy práctico, ¿no?" I commented on how unpractical it was. Did she think that we were going to stroll in the Retiro Park? That almost set her off.

Then she gave me a lovely gold bracelet she had bought for me, with these exact words:

"Y que no se entere tu hermano, ¿eh?" warning me that my brother better not find out. Now what did my brother have to do with the bracelet? Why couldn't my mother get something for me while he was living like a king, all expenses paid, in my parents' flat in Madrid? The minute my brother's name came up, my dad took my side and pronounced him a momma's boy.

"Inma tiene razón. Junior es un niño consentido."

Usually, one on one, my dad let my mother win; but with my help, at least he had a chance. Then my mother brought up all they were doing for me and for the baby too. Didn't I plan to go to Hawaii and leave them to babysit?

"¿Y ella? Que me quede yo con la niña, ¿no? Como si yo no estuviera enferma."

And had I even considered that she was sick and maybe it was too much for her?

We were at our dysfunctional best. Why couldn't we just tell the truth? We were all scared to death: my mother because her health kept failing and she thought her husband was having a lot more fun behind her back, and my dad because he couldn't face life alone and could see that his wife was not happy in the States nor living with him. As for myself, I feared that Paul would not return home from such an awful war. At that moment, I wished I had never come back to be near my parents. And when my mother brought up the eternal plaint that I had married too young—"Si no te hubieras casado tan joven"—I ended up yelling at the top of my lungs that I had married so young to get away from such an unbearable family: "Me casé tan joven porque sois todos una familia insoportable."

I wished then that Laura would never learn Spanish, as if she couldn't feel all the tension anyway. Why was it so difficult to love one's own family?

When I think about it now, I wonder why I hadn't gone back to school or gotten a part-time job since we didn't have a lot of money. When I was but seventeen years old, I tutored the college athletes in Spanish and worked in the bookstore while I went to school full-time. But the entire time Paul was in Vietnam, I felt almost paralyzed, unable to lead my own life and committed to take care of other people just the same. My mother was probably right after all. I had married too young.

My letters to Paul could not reveal my true feelings. I started faking a happiness I really didn't feel. I had the responsibility to keep my small family together, at least while he was overseas. Once in a while I'd get news that some of the couples we knew had separated or, much worse, that one of his classmates from Basic School had been killed. Paul wasn't the one to tell me, but somehow I found out. We were all telling our own stories but skipping some chapters. Just like Constance's albums don't mention one word about how the opposition to the war was growing in this country, there isn't a single article about the civilians who were being killed in Vietnam. As far as she was concerned, the My Lai massacre or the Tet Offensive never took place. Likewise, there isn't a picture of me crying in the baby album I kept for Paul nor a single image of the dark days I spent not listening to the news, but hearing and fearing what was happening over there. Whoever said that pictures don't lie?

I look at my mother-in-law's albums now, and I am amazed all over again. Just by reading the titles of the articles, one can deduce her outlook on the war: "Viet Switch Means More Troops Needed," "US Pilots Claim Three More MIGs," "Up Hill 881 with the Marines," "US Presents Reasons for Invasion of DMZ," "Mother

Says Fight to Win or Get Out," "Marines Slug It Out with Reds. Fighting Is Fierce in DMZ, Near Da Nang," "Vietnam: Slow, Tough but Coming Along," "B52s Round Out Second Year in Vietnam War," "US Marines Kill 589 Reds," "Death by Starlight" (about night flying), "Viet Floods Peril Marines" (during the monsoon rains). She underlined in red all the specific numbers of American casualties, of pilots shot down, of enemy wounded. She cut out maps, marking Chu Lai, Da Nang, Khe Sanh, Con Thien, Phu Bai, anyplace where Paul had been, charting the progress of the war chronologically as if she were the commanding general.

She also carried on a conversation with her absent son by writing questions and comments on the margins of the articles: "See Paul's letter of 5/29/67" (to confirm an experience Paul had written about); "Paul sent this clipping home. He remembered the pith helmet his father had given him!"; "Paul has slides" (referring to a particularly bloody battle); "Did you, Paul?" (wanting to know if he had gold in his survival gear); "Paul in Philippines O'Club heard call for men to proceed immediately to aid *Forrestal*" (about the fire on that carrier); "Paul agrees, but still is glad he is in the air rather than on ground—says the unadulterated terror can last only for minutes" (about flying over North Vietnam); "Some birthday present for Paul Jr.!" (when his base was hit by rockets). She had cut articles from *Time, Life, Wall Street Journal, New York Times,* in addition to the local papers. She even found articles in the press from the foreign countries she visited that year in Latin America: *La Prensa* in Lima, *El Mercurio* and *El Diario*

Ilustrado in Santiago de Chile, articles that made her son a hero in at least two languages.

One particular clipping, where I get mentioned, probably from the university paper, catches my eye: "5 Air Medals Garnered in 75 Missions." It says, "At last count received by his wife, Inmaculada, 400 N. River Road, he had flown 75 missions in F-4 Phantom jet fighters out of the marine base at Chu Lai on the Northern Coast of South Vietnam." Other members of the family also made news: "Capt. Davidson, a 1964 sociology graduate, is a son of Paul S. Davidson, dean of the business school, and Mrs. Davidson, South River Road. He has a seven-month-old daughter, Laura." Another leaves me absolutely speechless. It's from the bulletin of Saint John's Episcopal Church. It's true that we baptized Laura there before her father left for Vietnam, but Paul's zealous mother turned him into a "parishioner" who had by then earned "eight air medals, three special commendations and is now engaged in a ministry to the civilian population of South Vietnam."

XII

Of course, our first months of military life seem carefree compared to what we were going through later during the Vietnam War. When we lived in base housing, many of our basic needs were taken care of: utilities, maintenance, lawn service; and our family responsibilities were practically nonexistent then. The quarters were furnished in a very utilitarian way, so there was a big contrast between the Spartan furnishings and all the wedding gifts on display: the silver, china, and crystal my mother-in-law had insisted we register for, some art books, expensive table lamps, and even an original painting by Juan Genovés, a contemporary Spanish artist. Although we didn't have any money, there weren't many ways to spend it anyway. We actually got in trouble once when we had to borrow money from the credit union to pay the running tab at the officers' club, even though I don't drink. We did have our married friends over for cocktails or dinner quite often, and in every place we lived, there was always one bachelor or another who hung around.

George Bocock is one of the bachelors in residence who stands out in my mind. He was from Alabama and had the thickest Southern accent I had ever heard. Ironically, I had to repeat everything I said because he couldn't easily understand me either.

"What you just said?" he'd ask unintelligibly.

Virginia was the farthest he had ever been away from his home, and I was probably the first person from a foreign country he had met. Despite our communication problems, I could tell that he liked me. A burly, moody guy with a big round face and a crooked smile, George would come over on Saturdays to play chess with Paul. Sitting on the sofa, pretending to pay all his attention to the board, his eyes peeked above his eyeglasses, following me around as I moved through the apartment.

"George, have you ever had a serious girlfriend?" I asked him once.

"Nope. That's because I never met anyone like you," he answered.

I'm sure that the thought of being a married man with a warm wife ready to jump in the sack and a warm meal (served on matching Wedgwood dishes) waiting for him seemed unattainable. Paul was ready to share the latter with him, but not the former, although he enjoyed showing me off to him as one of his most valuable possessions.

"Isn't she the prettiest thing you ever saw?" he often said.

I was his wedding gift, so to speak, a precious object, his trophy wife, way before the term existed.

Sometimes George would join us on a day trip. Paul was a Civil War fanatic, and we visited several battlegrounds together: Fredericksburg, Manassas, Bull Run. There are several photos of George Bocock in our albums: going over the obstacle course wearing fatigues, with his helmet on and carrying a rifle, with a deer behind him in the Blue Ridge Mountains National Park, and in the guillotine in Williamsburg. It's all very sad now since he was our very first friend to be killed in Vietnam. Due to his poor eyesight, George didn't follow Paul's path to flight school. He remained a grunt and stepped on a mine near Da Nang. We didn't find out until months later, much too late to attend his funeral. We retired our chess set in his honor.

While we lived on the navy base in Pensacola, our apartment was on the third floor of some big World War II barracks that were going to be torn down. They had huge porches with wicker furniture and ceiling fans, the only place where we could sleep on hot nights. Just a few marines and their dependents were housed there since we were on temporary assignment while the men were in flight school earning their wings. I tried to get a job in the PX, which was within walking distance, even though Paul didn't want me to; but apparently, undocumented immigrants were not eligible.

"Sorry, ma'am. You are lucky to live in this base, and why would an officer's wife want to work anyway?" an NCO told me in a dismissive tone.

It turned out that I didn't have the proper visa to be in the United States. My student status had expired after we got married, and we hadn't lived long enough in one spot to establish residency. The closest consulate was in Mobile, Alabama, where we needed to file my papers, including a notarized translation of our Spanish wedding license. But it wasn't that easy, as if I didn't already know how complicated it was to become an American. When we finally got an appointment for the Tuesday after Labor Day, Hurricane Betsy was threatening the Gulf Coast. All the planes had been moved farther inland, and Paul had to leave with his squadron. The second time, I was in the navy hospital with an unexpected appendectomy. It was my first contact with dependent care, and not an appealing one, I might add. On the third try, it took us forever to get to the consulate because some of the roads were flooded from torrential rains. We were lucky to find anyone there. As it turned out, we had moved again before my visa could be approved. It took two more changes of address before the bureaucracy caught up with me in North Carolina.

By then I was already pregnant, and Paul was awaiting orders to go overseas. In the back of our minds, we did know that I hadn't resolved my visa situation; but understandably, we had bigger fish to fry, and the closest consulate was in Washington, DC. I remember that it was a sunny morning. I was sitting at the kitchen table, which faced the street, probably eating a BLT since I was always hungry, when I saw an unmarked white car stop right out in front, and two men dressed in civilian clothes got out. In spite of my youth, I managed to stay calm. I knew that it couldn't be bad news about Paul, although he was flying that day. He had left in his orange flight suit and his leather aviator jacket, but I hadn't heard the planes taking off yet, and we lived right next to the runway. Besides, these men didn't look like military personnel.

"Morning, ma'am. We are immigration officers," they told me. "Could you let us in? We've come in reference to your visa."

"I must see some identification," I said, not believing that they would show up, just like that, without calling us first.

"You must understand that in order to fly over North Vietnam, your husband needs top security clearance," the tallest one said. "He can't be married to an undocumented immigrant. We are here to facilitate the process." He explained all this in a loud voice, as if I were deaf because I have an accent, but I refrained from screaming back at him.

The other one spoke Spanish fairly well, albeit with an awful accent of his own. We read over all the documents I had with me, and ipso facto, I was transformed from an alien to a facilitator of war.

There were many other matters to take care of before Paul left for Vietnam: wills had to be made up (very sobering at such a young age), I had to take driving lessons (rather cumbersome in the third trimester of pregnancy), and preparations had to be made for the baby's arrival and the subsequent move to the Midwest.

The whole navy hospital experience was in and of itself an otherworldly ordeal, not that I had anything else to compare it to then. Once the doctor confirmed the pregnancy through a pelvic exam (this was before pregnancy tests), I was given a card with the dates of my appointments. At the scheduled times, I showed up in the obstetrics area, took a number, sat down, and waited to be called.

"Mrs. Paul Davidson, you're next." I almost didn't know they were calling me. It always took me by surprise when I heard my married American name.

Most of the women in the waiting room on my first visit were as young as I was or even younger, many with one or two kids already. Several of the mothers-to-be were Hispanic. While I hadn't seen any among the officers, I soon found out that it was very different in the enlisted ranks, where there were many Hispanics and African Americans. On a few occasions, I offered to translate for the young Latino women, knowing how lost they must have felt. We didn't have an assigned doctor, and we saw whoever was on duty that particular day, the better to be prepared for the delivery, my dear.

Before they left for Vietnam, the squadron was deployed in Okinawa for two months. Although he didn't like it, Paul agreed to remain behind since the baby's due date was fast approaching. But the baby's due date came and went, and we were still waiting at the base. As is known to happen with first babies, I was late. After a tense week—this time Paul came with me to my appointment—the doctor induced me and sent us home. We had no idea that this wasn't standard practice.

"Mrs. Davidson, be sure to shave so the corpsman won't have to do it later" was the only instruction I received.

Later that evening, when labor started and the contractions were getting regular, Paul dropped me off at the hospital because according to military regulations, soldiers were "only good for the launching pad." Then I was taken to my room and told to "have a good night." Alone in the room with the lights off, my water broke about an hour later, and I rang the bell for the corpsman to come. The baby's head was already showing as he wheeled me down the corridor to the labor room, screaming at the top of his lungs,

"Don't push, ma'am! Whatever you do, don't push yet!"

Even I knew that this wasn't standard operating procedure.

XIII

1300 31 July 1967

My dearest wife,

I cant remember if I have answered all your letters or not. As you know, I write to my family too, and I get my dates mixed up. Some days I am in a fog and cant focus my thoughts other than to get my job done and get back on the rack to dream about you. Maybe I should have asked for R&R earlier, now it seems like such a long time until the end of October.

Am now TAP to the group as S-2 briefer—good job—get to say when I will or won't fly. Am the fourth highest (out of sixteen RIO) in the squadron for the month in number of missions so still get to fly a lot. Have twenty missions for sixteen days total of eighty-three for two months and three weeks. When do I fly? At night. Have the highest night time of the squadron.

Sounds like my parents are really fixing up the cottage in Maine. I thought they wanted to get away from all that stuff. It sounds like they made the rounds of the relatives. They stayed with Uncle Freddy. Cindy has finished high school, wonder what she plans to do. When Doug finishes high school, it's the army for him, unless his father is afraid to have him handle a rifle.

Hope they take the offer to go to South America. Buenos Aires is supposed to be a beautiful city. Some of the air force officers going through survival in Panama with me were stationed in Buenos Aires, and they raved about it.

A while back, I met a guy in the O'Club, Bobby Atwood, who married Molly Malone, a girl in my class. He is an academy graduate and artillery officer. I just heard that he lost his commission over here for torturing a woman to death—just unfortunate that he got caught.

Too bad the apartment doesnt have a laundry room. Am glad you got diaper service if that helps you. You see, it's a good thing we didnt buy a washing machine before I left. You are such a natural for all the housekeeping things. I think the thing I hate most is doing my own wash. Don't mind making my rack every morning, keeping my area clean—but doing the wash is terrible.

It sounds like you will be happy to see your mother return. I think she likes me more than your father ever will. He must feel like I stole his little girl away.

Glad that Laura likes to go in the kiddy pool. I still think that she would be happier staying with Abuelita. Let's wait until she gets back to decide.

I too think of all the times we have been separated already, and you know that I miss you terribly. It does make for a lot of sweet reunions, though. Hawaii will be paradise, you'll see, my love,

Paul

2100 8 August 1967

Dearest Inma,

Glad you liked the wood things from the Philippines. I hear that Hong Kong is a real shoppers' paradise. I'll make sure to go after R&R. I want to get a reel-to-reel tape recorder. They are much cheaper than in the States, comparatively speaking. Be thinking what you want from there. It is supposed to have the biggest PX in the world!

Yes, we have hours of sheer boredom and minutes of sheer panic. It isnt really panic—it is pure, unadulterated terror. But it's the same on the ground or in the air, I am sure. In the air, though, it's only minutes or seconds while on the ground I can see a two—or three-hour firefight like one we just supported yesterday. A platoon had fifteen POWs in the jungle and were almost surrounded by VC. We were bombing an area so the platoon could get out and get to some helicopters. One of the most difficult missions I have ever seen. We were just plunking five-hundred-pound bombs in the jungle (no reference points, just tops of trees). I wouldnt want to be down there.

Your mother should be back by now. Let me know what's going on. Soon I will know some dates, and you can buy the plane tickets. Don't really understand why you want to stop in LA to see Adelle, but that's fine with me if it isnt too much more money.

Send more pictures of you too. I have lots of the baby.

Love you,
Paul

2000 27 August 1967

Dear Inma,

Sorry you and your parents are having a hard time. Here I thought you were dying to see your mother.

Remember to bring a measuring tape. No kidding, the men coming back from Hong Kong say that they can make a complete suit in just a few hours. You get to pick the material, style, everything top quality. A white silk suit sounds wonderful to me too. With your olive skin, it will look beautiful.

Poor Laura is teething, huh? I don't have anything against the pacifier, don't see why you are so upset. She looks like she is getting a bit more hair. She will be a brunette like her mommy. I guess, when we have a boy, he'll have blue eyes. A couple of the wives got knocked up during R&R. It doesnt seem too responsible to me. But it wont be for lack of trying!

I do think a lot about the meaning of this war. I just cant imagine that people in our own country don't understand what's going on. The big mistake is that Johnson continues to be president. He should tell people the whole story, spiff the war effort up, or be impeached. I sat down the other day and plotted two things. Number 1, where can an American walk safely unarmed in Vietnam: answer, US bases only. Number 2, areas more or less controlled by allied forces, my guess is we control 5-15 percent of the territory in I Corps. Simply, we are not winning this war in any way—let me change that, we are not winning the war in I Corps. The NVA and VC control all the highlands in the area—the point is, we cant beat the VC at their own game and must make it a strategic war where we can win.

I can understand why you dont want to see the news. I get angry just reading the magazines that get to us. It's even harder to think that all these smart-ass liberal people don't appreciate what we are doing over here.

I am not bored with your letters, never. I did notice the flowery smell of the yellow paper.

Miss you lots,
Paul

1700 11 September 1967

Dear Inma,

Dont be so worried about me. Am not interested in being a hero. Of course I want to be safe and come back home. I have learned some pretty sad things since being the S-2. A marine was in a village washing at the well. He was passing out candy and soup, etc., to the children, walked away from the well to a nearby wooded area, and noticed everyone became quiet, looked back over his shoulder and saw the people (three or four women and seven or eight kids) with their fingers in their ears. He looked down and saw a trick wire—he shot them all. Really don't care as long as I get out of this thing alive.

I have noticed that Vietnamese people don't have body hair, so the kids like to touch my hairy arms and they giggle. They call me "dawi," their word for captain. I do look at the children here sometimes and think about Laura. I have no idea how big she really is despite all the pictures you send. She's probably as tall already as a two-year-old Vietnamese kid.

I see Johnson wants to raise taxes. It says in our newspaper if he doesn't, we'll have a 23-billion-dollar deficit, and he predicted 8 billion. Oh well.

Enclosed is a money order for the tickets. This plus what you have saved should do it.

Not much new really, continue chugging along. Sometimes am so horny I could scream. I feel like climbing the walls. If I wasn't so busy, I would.

Lots of love to you and the baby,
Paul

XIV

If it wasn't enough to hear the Davidsons compare Vietnam to World War II, reminding me how lucky I was, my dad started reminiscing about his own war, telling us over our meals together of his heroic deeds.

"Papá, ¿no eras un operador de radio?" I asked, just to get the ball rolling.

Never mind that he was the radio communications guy and at times the cook, and that he never fired a single shot during the entire three years of the Spanish Civil War because of his poor eyesight. As a good Spaniard, eating is a fundamental need to be taken very seriously. "¿Te crees tú que se puede ganar una guerra sin comer?" (How do you think they could win the war without eating?)

And since the Republicans lost it, I guess he wasn't such a good cook after all, but I didn't dare say it out loud. Besides, their food supply was scarce from the time Franco isolated the southern front of Jaén where my dad was, so many times he had to make do with small animals—even snails—vegetables, or fruit they could find in the countryside. Once in a while, people in the neighboring towns would risk their lives providing staples—rice or flour—for the soldiers. My father made it sound as though it were a deed of biblical proportions.

"¡Ay, no exageres, Juanjo!" My mother was very quick to flag his exaggerations.

She had found that he'd made frequent outings to Lake Monroe while she was gone, and she had run out of patience with him. She had a sixth sense for knowing what was going on. I certainly didn't tell her. In fact, when she asked me if Lynn, one of his students, had been hanging around in her absence, I tried my best to reassure her, saying that Lynn was a rather zaftig woman and my father never liked his women overweight.

"Sí, es verdad no le gustan las gordas, pero le gustan mucho las rubias."

My mother was right again; my dad had always been crazy for blondes.

As long as I stayed in the kitchen with my mother while my father played with the baby in the living room, there was peace. So I started to cook Spanish food by default. Usually, she made a rice dish for the first course, not admitting that *Abuelito* loved it since they were angry at each other. It could be *Arroz al horno,* a casserole with bacon, chorizo, tomatoes, and chickpeas on top. On cold days, it would be *Arroz caldoso,* a souplike dish made with the broth from the *Cocido madrileño.* This traditional meat-and-vegetable stew from Madrid became the second course. Paella was de rigueur when they had guests and on many Sundays. It could be my favorite, an all-seafood paella or the classic one with chicken and pork. In either case, I could smell the saffron the moment Laura and I entered their place. To this day, I associate its unmistakable flavor and aroma with my mother. Saffron was sort of a kitchen timer in my family as well; when my mother had run out of it, it was time to go back to Spain. Never mind that some specialty shops in Indiana sold it; she thought it was never as fresh.

My mother always spoke in Spanish, even though she could understand some English, but for some strange reason, all the recipes I have from those months are written in English. In my eagerness to become more Americanized, I must have translated them as she spoke. Perhaps this was a way to get the American measurements, even if they were full of very Spanish instructions like "season to taste" or "cook until done." Since I knew how much Paul liked Spanish food, I had every intention to make all of them when he came back, in whatever new place the Marine Corps would send us.

My favorite recipe, however, was one for stuffed flank steak that my mother sent me in a letter when we were still living in North Carolina, before the baby was born. I have kept this long letter for many years, even if I have made the recipe only a couple of times. Its flavor can also be found in my mother's curly, unruly handwriting, in her warnings, and in her notes on social graces. If I close my eyes, I can even smell the saffron. On the day she wrote the letter, my parents were delayed at one of her doctor's appointments, and they got home quite late to eat: "Thank goodness I left the main course ready! Otherwise, today, your father's birthday, would have been a disaster." Here it goes in my own translation:

Abuelita's Carne Mechada

For the stuffing, *jamón serrano*, carrots cut lengthwise, a celery stick, pitted olives, cornichons, a small omelet with parsley, and a minced garlic clove. The stuffing should be in proportion to the cut of meat.

Ask the butcher to pound the flank steak and make sure that it isn't fatty. Arrange the ingredients of the stuffing prettily on the meat and roll it tight (be careful not to bunch the stuffing). Tie securely with a cooking string. Salt and pepper it.

For the sauce, one onion (if it's tender, otherwise skip it), diced carrots, three ripe tomatoes, some cracked pepper, and three garlic cloves.

Sauté the meat thoroughly, add sauce ingredients, and sauté as well. Cook at low heat until done, making sure that the broth doesn't reduce too much. I cook it for twenty minutes in the pressure cooker because it is faster (I know you are afraid of using it, but there isn't a problem if you read the instructions carefully).

Cook the rice with a little of the broth or a chicken cube (your father doesn't like white rice, and it is tastier this way).

Make the sauce by straining and mashing the cooked vegetables in the broth; add a little bit of sherry. Slice the meat and place prettily on a large oval platter. It can be served hot or cold (we like it at room temperature best).

Serve two ice cream scoops of the rice on each plate with two or three slices of the meat and cover with the sauce, which should always be warm.

Serve it with a green salad; and you have a complete, easy, delicious meal. If you have guests, they will lick their fingers. I made it for your in-laws once, and they raved about it.

With hugs and kisses for all,
Abuelita

The way I remember eating this dish as a child wasn't with rice but with French-fried potatoes cut in small squares, *patatas a cuadritos*, my brother's favorite. I guess my mother made the healthier change as a concession to her illness since she wasn't supposed to have fried foods. I never mastered the pressure cooker, but I did become very efficient at reading directions. In fact, the first meal I cooked for Paul as a married woman was "pork chops with apples and sauerkraut," from the recipes that came in our brand-new electric frying pan, which some practical soul must have given us as a wedding present. I don't think my mother would be very proud though, with my using only three ingredients and mixing sweet and sour flavors, something seldom done then in Spanish cooking.

Ironically, my mother, not my father, was the real victim of the Spanish Civil War. She had contracted hepatitis in the hospital where she volunteered during the three years Valencia was under siege, and she never fully recovered. Being the oldest of seven, she had to help with child care and household chores too from a very early age. Heaven only knows what they had to do to feed all those mouths! She had met my dad a few months before the beginning of the war. He used to say that he had never seen my mother alone, always with one or more of her siblings in tow, all handsome adolescents, all with wavy, thick reddish hair and light eyes like my mother's. By the time my dad left for the war, they had secretly planned to marry. In fact, three of her brothers also fought in the war, with the added bonus of having to reenlist in the service when Franco took over since they had been Republicans, the liberal ones in Spain, so their time fighting for the enemy didn't count. It's like a recessive gene that reappears in a family with each generation; it seems that we have all been blessed with one war or another.

XV

I arrived in Honolulu in some sort of a daze. I had planned to read and enjoy my solitude during the flights, but I kept wondering if my parents would be all right taking care of Laura. Although they knew her routine and she was used to them, I worried that having the baby for a full week might be too much for them, especially for my mother. I had never left Laura overnight before. Luckily, she was already eight months old and slept through the night, especially since she had started eating cereal and fruit. I was sure my mother would overfeed her or try something crazy, like potty training her, because she had already made some comments about how "at that age" I was almost trained, which I knew couldn't be true. Paul was right; if I was concerned about what might upset the baby, flying more than ten hours and staying in a hotel room with a strange man would be even worse.

During the short layover in the Los Angeles airport, I did notice that women's clothes had changed considerably from what I was used to seeing in Indiana. Everything was brighter and flashier, and the skirts were certainly much shorter. A lot of women wore tall white boots, just like the pictures of Twiggy I had seen in magazines. In any case, I was very conscious about my wardrobe because I was wearing maternity clothes almost until Paul left, and I knew how much he liked me to look sexy. I've always loved clothes, but I tend to be more classic than trendy. Just for this trip, I had bought several outfits: a new bikini with a hefty push-up bra, then in style, a long dress with spaghetti straps to wear over it, a short bright yellow dress but not a mini, a black cocktail dress, and of course, some provocative nightgowns. But then I wasn't sure it was all up to snuff, and I felt self-conscious.

Adelle and I had spoken on the phone and arranged a brief stopover to see her in Los Angeles on my way back.

"Oh, Inma, forget Jim! My new clothes were the best part of the trip!"

"Adelle, don't be funny. How can you say such things?" There I was, dying to see Paul. "Because Jim was literally a pain! Within twenty-four hours, I had one of my famous urinary tract infections, remember? Besides, we argued most of the time."

What would it be like seeing Paul? I bet he had changed a lot again, as it happened at the end of Officer Training School. During these last months, I had missed him terribly at first; but in some odd way, I was getting used to being alone and doing just what I wanted, setting the baby's schedule and my own. Except for my parents, there was no one to order me around anymore.

I must have fallen asleep in the last minutes of the flight. When I opened my eyes, I saw the bluest water I had ever gazed upon—a beautiful, bright blue, almost azure (*añil* in Spanish)—several islands covered with palm trees, and big puffy white clouds twirling around the plane. I could almost smell the warm air. At that moment, I started to feel a rush of excitement. I was covered with goose bumps, thinking of seeing and hugging Paul tightly in just a few hours.

When I got off the plane, the air was not only warm but also humid and moist. This was my first experience in a tropical climate, and it felt strange. I knew that Paul wouldn't be in Hawaii yet. There were all kinds of regulations we had to follow. The men were not allowed to wear uniforms while on leave in order to make themselves less conspicuous, as if they wouldn't be obvious anyway. The wives arrived first and checked with the military authorities who gave us a lei and took note of our hotel. They would contact us when our husbands were arriving. We could go and greet them at the air base or wait for them in our rooms. They would have a short briefing session first, and then we would be free for five days.

It was fun and exciting staying alone in a big, fancy hotel; I hadn't been in anything like this since our honeymoon in the Madrid Ritz. Our room had a wide view of Waikiki Beach and a small balcony. We had been afraid that R&R people would get crummy accommodations, but I thought this place couldn't be any better. The first day I slept a lot because I was exhausted. The next morning, on a whim, I decided to have my hair cut very short (that darn Twiggy again), even though I knew Paul loved my hair long. I felt dowdy wearing my hair in a bun, and I wanted to surprise him. And I sure would, since I looked so different I almost didn't recognize myself in the mirror. Then, in one of the boutiques at the hotel, I bought a combination of culottes and muumuu in bright blues and yellows—I can still picture it clearly, I kept it for so long. Some of the women ventured out to see the sights, but I sat by the pool and finally read a bit.

Late that evening, the phone startled me. Paul's flight was arriving at 0100. I hadn't imagined he'd come at that hour, so I was getting ready for bed, but decided to go to the base to meet him and made arrangements for a taxi to pick me up at the hotel. I really didn't know what to wear then; the evening was quite cool, and it seemed as if it would rain.

I didn't have any trouble recognizing Paul this time, so handsome and tall with a dark tan that emphasized his deep blue eyes.

"My god! What have you done to your hair!" were his very first words.

"Don't you like it? It's mod!"

"Mod? It must be as short as Laura's!"

"Listen, I have only my panties on underneath this trench coat," I whispered into his ear. He was speechless. It really was so unlike me. Outwardly at least, I was properly dressed, as always; but for once I was wearing the perfect outfit for him. Even with his tan, he looked completely flushed. For the first time in our marriage, I was ready to play out one of his fantasies.

We didn't have the greatest time, but it wasn't as bad as Adelle had predicted. It would have been better if I hadn't split open my knee on the first day when I hit a coral reef while bodysurfing in Waikiki Beach. They stitched me up in the hotel infirmary—so much for showing off my legs in the minidress. Here was Paul, unscathed after more than six months in Vietnam, and I injure myself on the very first afternoon of R&R!

"And no swimming for a few days, huh?" warned the doctor, as if we had a lot of time to spare. "No more bodysurfing either," he said, winking to Paul.

My knee throbbed, particularly that first night, but it didn't keep us from making love with gusto, compensating for all the time lost. I liked being naked with the curtains and the balcony doors open, feeling the breeze. There were many lights on the beach, and the moon, although not full, was bright. I could see the shining white of Paul's eyes staring at me.

"You are so beautiful to meee," he sang the words of our favorite song by Billy Preston softly in my ear.

Other nights we watched the sunsets on the beach or on our bed, kissing, licking, biting each other with the hunger of two war orphans. Once, we stood in the rain getting soaked like romantic-movie stars; my short hair was definitely more practical.

A highlight of the trip for Paul was visiting Pearl Harbor, the *Arizona* Memorial, and Wheeler Army Airfield, where we saw a P-40 fighter plane used in the movie *Tora, Tora, Tora*. "Those men were the real heroes," I remember him saying, marveling at the rudimentary aircraft.

Paul also loved the Battleship Missouri Memorial where the armistice of World War II was signed on September 2, which coincided with his own birthday.

"You realize that I was three years old when my father came back from the war? My mother and you really have a lot in common, don't you think?"

Yes and no, I thought. It was true that we both loved the same man.

"Do me a favor, Paul, don't get oedipal on me, okay?"

"Why do you always have to be so flippant? I thought you said you weren't going to piss me off."

"And you? You are the one comparing me to your mother, when you know it bugs me."

Everywhere we went, there were couples like us, on pseudo-honeymoons, holding hands and walking closely, if a bit awkwardly. We'd greet one another with smiles of recognition, without speaking, guarding the privacy of our precious moments together. My favorite day was when we took a drive alone around the island of Oahu, even though I had to sit in the back with my knee stretched out. We saw the Paiko Lagoon Wildlife Sanctuary, full of beautiful birds, and Hanauma Bay and Halona Cove, the beach where *From Here to Eternity* was filmed. We visited archaeological sites with ancient temples and looked at majestic volcanoes in the distance. We did many of the touristy things, including a luau, where we danced the hula (my knee was stiff, but I could move my arms) and ate the traditional roasted pig.

One evening, we went to a nearby hotel to hear Don Ho, the hottest entertainer then, and had our picture taken with him. I sang along when he played "Tiny Bubbles" and cried—I hate to admit it—during the "Hawaiian Wedding Song."

"Don't cry, baby!" Paul admonished. "Time is going to fly by. You'll see, I'll be home before you know it."

Yes, my clothes worked out just fine. Paul stopped complaining about my short haircut, not that he was a fine one to talk, since his head had been shaved during the last four years.

"You haven't said much about the war," I commented toward the end of the trip.

"I don't really want to. It's a miracle I have been able to put it out of my mind for a few days. You rambled on incessantly about the baby, though." As if I wasn't paying enough attention to him.

I could see that he had changed somehow, hardened already. Deep inside his blue eyes, there was an expression I hadn't seen before. He did talk constantly about his buddies, but he had always done that. He was the one who acted like his mother, the gazetteer.

On our last night together, I woke up and couldn't get back to sleep. I lay there next to him, listening to his rhythmic breathing, and felt lucky that he was alive and peaceful for the time being. We had made love earlier, and he was barely awake when we said good night.

"You sure are wasted!" I teased him.

"Of course, because I've done all the work," he replied.

Knowing that he had an early flight the next day, I didn't want to wake him. But I don't remember wanting him so much ever before in our life together. I rubbed my pelvis up and down his butt and turned him over on his back when I felt him stirring. Neither one of us spoke a single word. I started stroking his little soldier, *soldadito*—that's what I always called it—until it stood at attention. Paul kept his eyes closed, but I opened mine wide, as if photographing every second we had left together. I sat on top of him with ease, still wet from our previous encounter. I rode him hard and steady while he held my breasts tight in his hands.

"Now who's doing all the work? Huh, big soldier?" Ah, the pleasure of laughter in the middle of the night!

XVI

If anything, the months following R&R were the most difficult to bear. To continue with the movie theme, it would have been similar to *A Taste of Honey*, which Paul and I had seen on one of our first dates. After a few days in his company, I missed Paul more than ever but was inexplicably angry with him at the same time. I just wanted a "normal" marriage, whatever that was, not this arrangement, the constant worry and detachment I felt. On the surface, everything was fine; Laura and the *Abuelitos* had gotten along well, my stitches had come out, and the knee was healing and Paul's letters had started coming again. But here I was stuck in limbo, writing letters and waiting. I knew better than to keep complaining to my family; *Abuelita* was feeling weaker, and her liver function tests were alarming. My parents had decided that during the week of Thanksgiving, they were going to visit the Mayo Clinic, where they might be able to start my mother on a new experimental treatment.

I've never understood Thanksgiving Day, and it isn't just because we don't have anything like that in Spain. Why commemorate the subjugation, disappearance, and the near-genocide of the American natives? I guess I was politically correct before it was in vogue. It would be like celebrating Columbus Day in my country. In fact, October 12 is a holiday anyway, the day of the *Virgen del Pilar*. My family barely celebrated Thanksgiving in the United States, and then only if someone invited us; otherwise, we just took the day off like everyone else, but without the whole rigmarole of the turkey and stuffing or, worse yet, the pumpkin pie, which, since Laura had been born, my father compared to baby shit. I still can't figure out why the menu is identical every year. With the same food and the same family, it's impossible to even tell the years apart. Except for that year.

In my grouchy state of mind and with my parents away at the Mayo Clinic, I informed the Davidsons that I wouldn't spend Thanksgiving with them. Usually, they made a huge production out of it, displaying the entire collection of silver, finest china, and crystal regalia; inviting a number of friends and relatives; and issuing last-minute invitations to neighbors who might otherwise be spending the day alone.

"But you have so many things to be thankful for, dear" was my mother-in-law's instant remark. "Besides, Michael is coming home from Ohio, and he would love to see you and the baby."

"Why can't you understand that I prefer to be alone with Laura as if it were any other day?" I said. "Then I won't miss Paul as much."

What I didn't tell her was that seeing Michael home from the National Guard, while his brother was in Vietnam, made me miss him all the more and feel angry too.

"Suit yourself, Inmaculada, dear." My mother-in-law didn't persist in her criticism. Perhaps they had one more reason to be thankful for my not joining them; I couldn't have been very good company in those days.

On Thanksgiving evening, when I was peacefully writing to Paul, Constance called to let me know that Michael would stop by to see the baby and bring me some delicious leftovers, another absurdity to us Spaniards. It was almost Laura's bedtime, but he did get to see her awake long enough to say, "She's adorable. She looks just like her father."

"But she has my coloring, don't you think?" I could tell that he wasn't into babies at all.

Much to my surprise, Michael stayed and chatted for a while before joining his friends in town. We had hardly seen each other since we were freshmen in college together. Sometimes I wondered if we would have been better friends had he not introduced me to his older brother, who made it clear that he was smitten with me at first sight and that meant hands off to the younger brother.

"I can't believe you haven't kept in touch with the people in our class." He sounded so sophomoric. I felt years away from college.

"Well, you know that I didn't graduate . . . and besides, they are against the war," I said as an excuse.

"But so are you, aren't you?" he probed, but I didn't want to talk with him about it.

He filled me in about a whole list of people whose names sounded barely familiar. Not one of them was in Vietnam. A few had even filed as conscientious objectors, and some were already married too.

"You remember your friend Lynda, the blonde with the Thunderbird convertible? She didn't finish her degree either. She eloped and is already divorced, living in Texas somewhere."

"Oh, yes, I remember her." But I was really thinking, what's the story with these Davidsons, always keeping track of people they know, reporting their failures?

"How did you manage to stay away from the war, Michael? Why wasn't your brother so lucky?" I finally asked, full of resentment.

"Well, you know how it is with the sons of veterans from World War II. Only the oldest is the privileged one. It's like a rite of passage for them." He had the whole issue rationalized to his advantage.

"Oh, really? How fortunate for you!"

I thought I'd be glad to have a chance to talk with someone my own age, but our conversation was strained, as if we hadn't a thing in common anymore. If we kept talking about the war, we would end up arguing. I offered to show him the pictures from R&R, but he suddenly got up to leave. His friends would be wondering where he was.

"Enjoy the turkey, it's delicious!" he said as he left.

And it actually wasn't so bad. The stuffing and the sweet potatoes were really quite tasty, even if I had to eat alone.

Michael's visit evoked in me all kinds of memories. He was very different from his brother, not nearly as handsome as Paul, much shorter, and with a lazy eye that was very distracting if one wasn't used to it. He always had a sense for business, though, and even when we were in college, he earned a pretty penny giving horseback-riding lessons at a nearby horse farm. The Davidsons had always kept horses; Bourbon and Anisette were the ones I remember. Michael had dreamed of being in the Olympics someday. Back when I was trying to ingratiate myself into their family, I took riding lessons from him. I wonder if I looked like a proper daughter-in-law-to-be with my velvet helmet, riding English style.

In fact, although I didn't even know at the time, I lost my virginity, so to speak, on Anisette. I was not a confident rider, and I never got over being afraid of horses. As I said, I did it all to earn some stars. One fall afternoon, after Paul had already left for Officer Training, we were riding in the paddock, practicing my cantering form, when Anisette got spooked by the wind and took off running. I was so startled that I couldn't hold on to the reins and was thrown over the fence. Michael was furious with me.

"You have to get back on the horse and ride him to the stable. You need to show him who's boss and get over being afraid once and for all," he screamed.

I was quite sore—and embarrassed too—but as soon as I could tell that I wasn't seriously hurt, I made a promise to myself that I would take no more horseback-riding lessons for the rest of my life.

When I got to my dorm and checked for bumps and bruises, I thought it was odd that I had a bright bloodstain in my panties, although it wasn't time for my period. Only during the honeymoon night, when I hadn't experienced the expected pain and the telltale spotting, did I realize what must have happened and then tried to explain it to Paul. He wasn't much more experienced than I was and didn't press for more information, although he teased me.

"My, you are learning fast! That's an old American tale." But I think he believed me.

For all the loneliness I was feeling that Thanksgiving, I wish I had lost my virginity in a more traditional way—in Paul's arms, before we were married, making love wildly or more romantically, on our wedding night.

I had all kinds of strange dreams that Thanksgiving night. It seemed that just when Laura had started to sleep longer, I was often restless. I could fall asleep if I read for a good while, but once I woke up—for whatever reason, no matter what time it was—the night was over for me. In my dream, I fall off a horse again. It isn't Bourbon or Anisette, for this horse is smaller and has white fur. Even so, I know I don't want to ride it anymore. Instead of being thrown to the ground, I end up rolling on top of a bed. Both Paul and Michael are there staring at me, but I'm not sure it is them because both have long hair and neither one is wearing a military uniform. Then, all of a sudden, I am in a white nightgown and Paul and I are making love (I hope it was Paul!). I can't reach orgasm because I'm cold, and I keep asking him to wait for me, that I will come, to be patient, that I don't want him to stop . . .

When I wake up, it's cold for real. The covers have slipped off the bed, and the pillow is between my legs. Several hours of thinking and worrying await me.

XVII

1500 13 November 1967

Dearest Inma,

I can still smell you on my skin and my civvies. It's been hard to concentrate since I got back. Send me some pictures right away. Want to show everyone my hot wife. Don't be angry with me. I told some of the men about your stunt with the raincoat, and they think you are quite a sexy lady. Cant believe that you cut your hair (no, it didnt look like a helmet before), but you looked great even with your hair short, now don't cut it again until I get home, okay?

Guess I got some rest, but don't feel too relaxed. No sooner did I get back than I was told I am no longer the S-2 briefer, seems I was just filling in. So what happens now? There is a vacancy in the civic affairs office. I'm qualified with my background in sociology. It is up to the squadron CO. I could fly full-time and only spend two or three mornings a week on this job. I want it, but I may be labeled as a shit bird for wanting to do something else besides fly all the time.

I bet the holidays are going to be difficult here too. I have a chance to go to Hong Kong and Saigon, which should help make the time fly (funny, huh?).

Did you think I forgot? Happy birthday to you! It was good that we celebrated it in Hawaii, don't you think?

Tell me what the relatives say about me in the R&R photos. Did everyone like their gifts? How's your mom feeling? How's your knee doing? Wonder if they have Purple Hearts for dependents . . . All in all, I think we had a terrific time.

Kisses for the baby. Missing you lots, yours,

Paul

2300 24 November 1967

Dear wife,

Still no letters from you, then I'll get a bunch together. Not surprising, things seem to be falling apart here. I told you about the job I'm really interested in. You know, if you don't want to fly all the time, you are labeled as some kind of turd. I am getting tired of bouncing around from one thing to another, all I've gotten out of this outfit is crappy deals. Oh well, my EAS is 1 May '69.

Personnel admin and planning in the MarCor are nil. I hope they fall flat on their face. Our squadron has one vehicle, we have to borrow a truck from the army to haul our bombs. When we came from Japan, we brought a truck with us we got from air force salvage, a metro. An order came through that all vehicles obtained in this manner had to be turned in to be destroyed as they were being operated on appropriated funds. I couldnt believe it. Using too much gas and of course, no vehicles to replace them.

I hope I have the opportunity to speak when I get home, it probably will be only once. The whole affair seems like a bunch of overgrown kids flying around dumping bombs with absolutely no purpose in mind.

Well, no more for today. Will write tomorrow in a better mood, I hope.

Love you, no change there,
Paul

PS: Have a great Thanksgiving with everyone!

2100 8 December 1967

Dear Inmaculada,

I bet you didn't think I would remember. Happy Saints' Day, sweetheart. I think it's so Spanish that you still celebrate it, and I do love your complete name, even if I don't use it much, Inmaculada Concepción. Bet there isn't anyone here with a wife like you.

Yes, I do like my new job. Usually, I go with two other men and an interpreter into a so-called friendly village, our weapons loaded. We are trying to win the people's friendship, but must be prepared for ambush. Sometimes a child will be waiting for our jeep and says, "No sweat today, dawi," the friendly Viet term for captain. In one village I'm overseeing the construction of a schoolhouse. I guess mending is better than mauling. The native workers give us American soft drinks because they know we like them. I don't dare refuse it, but I always take a little sip first, gingerly.

We did have some excitement a few days ago with the VC attack on a district headquarters a few miles away from here. Was quite a victory. Around one hundred VCs were killed or wounded. The president of Vietnam came up to congratulate the chief. The Vietnamese did the fighting themselves, which is quite unusual. Things seem to be heating up around here. We were supposed to get a truce for Christmas and Tet, the Vietnamese New Year. We will see.

The weather has been unbelievable. It will rain like the monsoons are supposed to for three, maybe four days, and then it will clear and be nice and cool and sunny. The monsoons are supposed to be next to unbearable, but they have been pleasant so far. Knock on wood.

Should be going to Hong Kong any day now. Will get your silk suit and hope to do some more shopping for the holidays.

Give my love to everyone. I miss you all,

Paul

2100 21 December 1967

My dearest Inma,

Thanks for the cheeses and the cigars. It all arrived in good shape. Will share it with some of the men on Christmas and New Year. Tell my mother the packages and checks arrived too. Some of the money went for a party, and the rest is being used as scholarships to send children to school. It takes about five dollars to send a child to school for a month. This buys him books and supplies as well as putting a little money in his parents' pockets in order to let him go to school instead of putting him to work.

The Vietnamese are funny. When they realized that my men were not going to build the dispensary by themselves, they finally got busy and began to work. Then I was told to make a dedication speech and make it long, or else people will think that the dispensary was not any good.

Have asked to be stationed at El Toro in Camp Pendleton, California, like we spoke about during R&R. Yes, it's far from our parents, but it may be our only chance to live over there. After our discussion, Im beginning to worry about what to do when I get out of the marines. It's less than two years away, can you believe it?

I heard that Peter P. is going to Thailand. They have F-4s in Ubon and Nakhon Phanom. Ubon is our divert base in case of bad weather. We like to go there for a little R&R. The air force bases are just like being in the US. Oh well, maybe the marines will catch up someday. I will be sending a thank-you letter to the church. There is time for one more package before I leave for Saigon. After that am training the new civic affairs officer and I am on my way home.

I can see an end to this year coming up. I try not to think about it too much, or I get delusional. Back home (don't know where yet) with you and little Laura. Can't believe that she is walking and talking. You are the best mommy in the world. She must love you so much.

As I do,
Paul

PS: Almost forgot. Have a good family Christmas. Don't get presents for me, it makes me superstitious. All I want is to get back there.

XVIII

Both of my parents had the ability to transform the mood of the household when they were happy—my mother in particular. Not only had they been able to stabilize her condition at the Mayo Clinic, but my brother also announced he would come to spend the Christmas holidays, and that cheered her up to no end. I hadn't seen my brother since my wedding in Madrid three years earlier. We really didn't have direct contact, always getting each other's news through my parents. I thought he was a rather spoiled young man. He was in his late twenties, without a job, going to the university full-time, where he had changed majors several times. All his bills were paid by our parents, although this situation was not so unusual in Spain. Nevertheless, I was excited to see him. I wanted to show Laura off and impress him with the maturity of my married life, even if I was flying solo at the time.

Laura was beginning to walk and say a few words. She was turning into a sweet, funny kid whose personality was starting to show. She called my mother *Litaaa* and my father *Litooo* because they corrected her when she didn't use the proper Spanish ending. Imagine, and she wasn't even a year old!

"Abuelito, la palabra perfecta con las cinco vocales." Did my father really expect me to teach her the five vowels in Spanish already?

Laura was so used to playing alone that on the rare occasion when we had more than a couple of people over, she liked going to her room, jumping headfirst into her playpen. She had also learned to get her father's picture and kiss it when she heard the word *daddy* mentioned, as if she understood what a father was. In some ways, she looked like him, with large features, almost too large for a baby's face, and deep-set eyes, although not blue like his. But her already serious demeanor was typically Spanish. She knew that she was the one and only little princess in the realm, always dressed a bit too formally, with matching sweaters made by her adoring *Abuelita*. My mother used to comb Laura's hair in tiny corkscrew ponytails, since she still didn't have much hair, with huge and stiff bows that certainly made her look like an immigrant. I loved Laura's smell, a mixture of my mother's sweet, clean scent—who was always hugging her—and Nenuco, the baby cologne she had brought from Madrid especially for the baby.

I was looking forward to Christmas, even though we had agreed to go to the Davidsons for dinner. Other than Laura's first birthday, which was just around the corner, it was the last holiday before Paul's date to come home. I could hardly hide my anticipation. I had started to fantasize about the moment of his arrival. Usually, I could fall asleep imagining all the details: the plane landing, his tall figure coming down the stairs, hugging him tightly inside the terminal, getting into the car holding hands, entering the apartment, closing the door behind us, collapsing on the bed with little Laura between us, finally a family of three together.

When my brother arrived, I was amazed to see that not only was his face still covered with zits but also that despite the chunky combat boots he had on, I had grown a couple of inches taller than him, much to his consternation. He wore some strange combination of ranger jacket and camouflage pants he had bought in an army surplus store, thinking he looked like Che Guevara, whereas they really made him look like a hobo. I could tell right away that we had grown farther apart than I had imagined. He spent entire days outfitting himself for tennis as if he were going to play in Wimbledon. He bought a new set of luggage, a waterproof watch, and the latest camera available with two different lenses. He spoke English with a fake British accent (talk about camouflage!). I accompanied him on a couple of his shopping expeditions, but seeing him use my dad's credit card gave me an upset stomach, so I left him to our loving mother for companionship. Luckily, *Abuelita's* meals were even tastier than usual when he was visiting; the poor lad had not eaten a home-cooked meal in ages.

"¡Ay, el pobre no tiene quien le haga una buena comidita!"

No comment from me there. I had decided to keep my mouth shut to have some peace. I feared telling them what I was really thinking.

To commemorate the approaching holidays, I pulled from the back of the closet some of the Christmas decorations Paul and I had bought the year before in North

Carolina when we were awaiting the baby's arrival. Like this year, I hadn't wanted to decorate then either—with Paul's deployment menacing our lives—but at the last possible moment, we went to the local drugstore and bought a few boxes they had lying around, some of them discounted because they were half open. This time, Laura and I ventured out through the snow and bought a small but very fragrant tree, which I set on a table high enough so she wouldn't get into trouble. I even put in the tree a string of blinking lights by myself.

My brother was driving the ferocious Cougar when they picked us up on Christmas Day. I could see that it was back to the old hierarchical order: the men in front, the ladies in back. My brother was wearing a formal dark suit with a white shirt and a red tie. With his hair smoothed to one side, he looked to me exactly like the famous Spanish bullfighter.

"Oye, si te pareces muchísimo al Cordobés." So much for keeping my mouth shut.

My father kept giving directions to my brother on how to drive in the snow.

"Oye, oye, oye, cuidadito con la nieve, ¿eh?" Junior didn't appreciate it since he considered himself an expert on every subject; never mind that it rarely snows in Madrid. I could feel the tension between them already. Besides, during my brother's stay, my dad had to curtail his students' visits. Junior also liked blondes, and I'm sure my dad feared the competition. No wonder my mother loved having her son around!

The snow had fallen a couple of days before and covered the frozen river, with the winds making some small mounds that twirled like ethereal ballerinas on a mirror. Suddenly, regardless of the dynamics inside the car, I became aware of the beauty of the day. It was mostly cloudy, but the sun would peek brightly from between the fast-moving clouds, reflecting shining, fleeting sparks of light from the water. The huge trees looked skinny and light swaying in the wind without their leaves. What had happened to me? I suddenly realized that I hadn't even appreciated the change of seasons, which I love and had missed so while living in the South. Where had the fall, my favorite time of the year, gone? Indiana could be beautiful even without Paul, as this frozen river road certainly was on this crisp winter day.

Laura had fallen asleep sitting on my lap, wrapped in her fancy, furry Spanish coat, and I could feel her warmth against my chest. This was probably as warm and close as I could ever be with my family, imperfect as it was.

My dad continued his warnings to my brother.

"Oye, oye, oye, cuidado con el hielo en la carretera." (There could be a frozen patch on the road.)

"Papá, por Dios, no seas tan pesado."

This confirmed it. I would not teach Spanish to Laura so she wouldn't have to hear her uncle calling his own father an awful pest.

The houses, trimmed in green and red, looked inviting standing in the snow with smoke coming out of their chimneys. Somehow, the snow had changed their appearance into whimsical shapes. Before turning into the Davidsons' driveway, we spotted Bourbon and Anisette, their hair turned into a thick coat ready for winter, standing by the fence with smoke steaming out of their noses, as if they sensed we were coming. Walter, the old golden lab, started to bark and follow our car as soon as we turned the corner; he definitely knew that company had arrived.

The Davidsons always went all out for the holidays. *Mère,* the old matriarch, had prepared a stuffed goose and all kinds of sweets she thought my parents would like. The table was set in their best English china and antique crystal (nerve-racking with an eleven-month-old around). The Christmas tree, standing between the front windows, was so huge that it almost covered the view of the river. Piles of wrapped presents were gathered under the tree, and there were opened ones tucked in every corner. I had tried several times to explain to them that in Spain we don't give presents on Christmas Day, and that on January 6, only the children get them.

"The three Wise Men, *Los Reyes Magos*, bring them. Don't you remember, Connie, when you came for Paul's and my wedding?"

"Yes, dear. That's right, and tomorrow is your wedding anniversary." At least she had remembered that.

I have since given up on the Old World traditions; Christmas is an American holiday, Davidsons' style, period. Forget doing anything with the kings in January.

I am sure we brought gifts for them. They had even thought of my brother, giving him a Cross pen and pencil set, I guess in case he ever became an executive. Laura spent the day opening toys and hadn't finished by the time we left. We saved Paul's gifts, unopened, for his return.

I heard my parents making funny remarks in Spanish about the Davidsons, one of them being "Tienen de todo, menos un buen vino." (They have everything but a decent wine.)

I wasn't part of their jokes that day. I had brought my camera and went around taking pictures of the occasion. The perfect way to be present and detached at the same time—my specialty. I could see through a different lens that the Davidsons—no matter how traditional—were generous, loving people; they just wanted a family as much as I did. You'd think that Paul's and my parents would get along better. After all, both fathers worked in the same university. It was the stupid war that was separating us, each of us looking at it from our individual perspective.

Laura and I took a nap upstairs in Paul's old room under the eaves. It was almost as he had left it when he joined the marines: Hemingway's complete novels on the desk, some horseback-riding trophies on the shelves, even his high school yearbook still there on the top shelf. On the night table was a picture of the two of us standing by the old MG—I look like a child—and his college graduation picture, exactly the way I remember him when we first fell in love. He had such a tender gaze in his eyes then.

"Look, Laura, your daddy!" And she bent over it, giving him a kiss.

XIX

    While I rooted around in the closet putting away the Christmas decorations, I found a folder with a dozen or so black-and-white publicity photos of chorus girls from Las Vegas. One was inscribed "To Paul, good luck to you" or something like that; it was hard to read the scribble. He must have brought them when he went to Twentynine Palms, in California, for one of the survival schools. I seemed to remember that the squadron had stopped in Vegas. The stupid pictures almost ruined my good mood again. I was jealous and angry. Here I was counting the days before he got home, and now this.

    I was sure that if I could ask Paul, he would laugh it off and call me silly—that these weren't any different from the pictures we had taken with Don Ho in Honolulu during R&R. But to me they were different; I hadn't hidden those from him in some closet. I wondered then if Paul had missed us during the holidays as much as I had missed him. I know that for days, my letters were somewhat curt because he had commented on that already. The fact is that the news coming out of Vietnam then was so upsetting I thought better of telling him about the girlie photos, filing my hurt away with all my other complaints to keep the truce a while longer.

When I look at my mother-in-law's albums again, the suspicions I had then about her hawkish ways are confirmed: "War Resumes in Vietnam," "Marines, Reds in Bunker Fight," "N. Viet Troops Pound US Marines," "Allied Troops Shelled; Jets Bomb Railroad," "Yank POW Killings Bared," "US Bombers Blast Hanoi Area Targets," "US Jets Use Break in Rain to Hit North," "Marines in Fierce Battle." The statistics for 1967 were nothing but alarming: "26 Yanks Died Daily in Viet War" and "170 Wounded Each Day."

Despite the fact that the campus demonstrations seemed to have quieted down with the cold weather, I had an uneasy feeling that something could happen at the end of Paul's tour of duty. I was proud of him working with the Vietnamese people, but I kept thinking—thanks to the general in North Carolina—that being in the air was safer. I pretended not to read the papers, but I still devoured *Time* and had started turning on the evening news while feeding Laura.

During one of my father-in-law's visits, I broached the topic.

"Dad, I'm so worried. Don't you think that Paul was safer flying all the time?"

"When you spend eight months bombing a place apart, it's nice to get a chance to put it back together again," he said. "I would have liked to do the same when I was a marine, but there were no villages left after we bombed the South Pacific Islands . . ."

He really couldn't answer my question. His son's experiences were making him relive his own, although their personal involvement was not the same. Every war is alike on the surface but painfully unique at the same time.

"Besides, all leathernecks need to be assigned to ground duty so they can learn the life of the sweaty, earthbound infantry grunt," the old colonel added.

Amazingly, I managed to forget about the Las Vegas photos by working with my mother-in-law collecting gifts for the Vietnamese children's upcoming Tet holiday, their new year, which in 1968 marked the year of the sheep. She made up a circular and mailed it with the church bulletin, always happy to get the family name in print. They could use unbreakable plastic toys; squeeze dolls or animals; all kinds of school supplies like pencils, crayons, tablets, and rulers; and items for personal hygiene such as soap, toothpaste, combs, DDT powder, and laundry soap. Lightweight new clothes in all children's sizes were also needed. Personal checks could be made out to Captain Paul Davidson in his role of civic affairs officer. Parcels could be mailed to the Fleet Post Office in San Francisco. I was really touched when Paul's interpreter sent some tiny silk sleepers for Laura that were already much too small for her. And to think of all the toys and clothing she had!

Laura's first birthday party was a quiet, private family affair, but with all the usual bellicose undertones. *Mère*, in one of her rare outings, arrived with the grandparents. Her surprise gift consisted of the certificate, sealed and framed, that made Laura a daughter of the American Revolution. I found out that one of *Mère's* French ancestors had the necessary illustrious pedigree. Her grandfather, I believe, had also fought in the American Civil War. Proudly, she was passing on to the baby an antique writing box that he had carried with him.

"Oh my, the writing box is beautiful!" I said. "But do you think it's appropriate for a first birthday?" Family history is one thing, but I found this obsession with war appalling.

"Inmaculada, dear, don't be so touchy. Be glad that your daughter is part of such a distinguished tradition." My mother-in-law was probably behind this honor too.

I wonder if this meant that Paul was no longer disappointed about having had a daughter instead of a son. I couldn't wait to ask him. There I was, feeling angry at him again.

The *Abuelitos* brought along some old friends who were visiting from Madrid. Kai, a neighbor from down the hall, was there as well, Laura's only friend her own age. Just because I've seen the home movie many times do I recall any of this. At some point, Laura jumped into her playpen, as if wanting some peace and quiet. I imagine my parents stayed late chatting with their friends. What has especially remained in my memory is that when everyone was gone, I turned on the TV and saw the screen light up as if with fireworks. The American embassy in Saigon had been attacked by a suicide raid. The entire city was under siege. The Tet Offensive had begun.

I ran to the bedroom to check Paul's letters and see if he had given me a date for his upcoming trip to Saigon, but I was sure he was already there. Besides, the report said that all the bases south of the DMZ, including Chu Lai, were being hit relentlessly. No wonder I had felt such a feeling of doom. I didn't dare make a phone call to my in-laws for fear that someone more important might try to call me, since those were the days before call-waiting. I lay on the bed with the lights on, expecting the worst. I must have just fallen asleep when Laura woke up in the early morning. Nothing, still no news. I called my mother-in-law first.

"Inmaculada, dear. Don't be so upset. You would have heard already if anything had happened. I'm sure Paul is all right," Constance, always in control of her emotions, tried to reassure me.

"I'll tell Grandfather to come by and see you at lunchtime. Maybe he can contact General Chapman, the new marine commandant. They're old friends."

Adelle hadn't heard from Jim, either. Although our husbands were no longer in the same squadron, I was hoping she knew something more than I did.

"I don't even think there's phone communication," she told me when I called. But she too was worried enough to have stayed home from school that day.

XX

Dear wifey,

Glad that the suit fits you. Bet you look great in it, all in white. I did notice the buttons, very unusual, I agree. Don't be silly—wear the Mikimoto pearls to your heart's content. They are supposed to be the best in the world and last a lifetime. You'll just need to have them restrung sometime, but that's all. The ones I got for my mother are not the same quality as yours.

I got myself a flak jacket with a nice collar. I can squinch up like a turtle when I have my helmet on so nothing is exposed except my nose and mouth, feels more secure that way.

Haven't flown in a few weeks. Miss it. I now have more than 150 missions. Things from the air always look so much prettier, even in this country. Up close, the towns are destroyed with squatters everywhere building shacks amid scattered piles of litter. Besides, it stinks of TNT, decay, and death. As much in the mind as in the nose.

I hear that R. Higgings is dropping a few courses here and there—draft his ass. He and all the other college kids could learn a thing or two over here. They dont know what's going on. Take good care of yourself now. I have started packing my trunk, Big Bertha. It's going directly to California. Dont worry, I'm keeping most of my civilian clothes with me to wear at home, and I won't get another haircut for a while. I'll be there soon to take care of you in more ways than one.

All my love,
Paul

2120 5 February 1968

Dearest Inma,

Well, looks like the real war has begun over here. You must have heard that Chu Lai was rocketed on the morning of Laura's first birthday. I was asleep when the first rocket hit the aircraft revetments. I knew what it was instantly and ran out the front door to the bunker and saw the airplanes on fire. For a moment, I froze. I couldn't believe we were getting it. If I could have shrunk to less than a cubic inch, I would gladly have done so. I have never felt so helpless or scared in my life while those rockets fell all around. The VC were trying for the aircraft, and the company grade huts are in direct line with the revetments. Our closest bunker was thirty yards away. Man, do they go off with a bang! One bunker took a direct hit that killed three of the men. In all we took forty-eight rounds during twenty minutes. Sort of caught everyone with their pants down.

The next day, I did some snooping and pooping and found out from army intelligence that we also had a buildup in the area like everywhere else. Still have three or four battalions. One of them is the 308th Mountain Artillery Battalion that came down from Da Nang. I think we can thank them for the rockets.

Now civic action has been curtailed throughout the I Corps area. I have been helping the S-2. I made a couple of night intelligence snatches. An informant sets up a meeting time and place where he can meet with me to pass on any movements the VC are making at night. It is kind of scary, but I know the information broke up two attempted terrorist raids on two different towns and one night resulted in H&I fires that killed at least five and wounded many more.

During the daytime, I have been to a couple of hamlets where I didn't recognize half of the men who were gathered in the squares. One unit in the area has a ten-year-old boy fighting with it. It is kind of sad because the young fellow is in for a rough time if the PFs catch him. I guess he can kill as well as his older brethren.

How is everyone viewing the recent Tet Offensive? Do people really think we should stop the bombing to see if North Vietnam will talk peace? I am sure they do. However, remind them of the Tet truce this year.

Am I glad to be getting away from this place or what? Am literally counting the days.

Love to all and to you and to Laura,
Paul

XXI

Paul called from San Francisco on the evening of March 13, sounding so far away; it was hard to believe that he was no longer in Vietnam.

"Paul, sweetheart," I kept repeating through my tears, "I'm so relieved and so happy."

"Let everyone know, but I don't want anyone else in the airport, just you. I'm really exhausted, and I have another day of flying to get there."

"Are you sure?"

"Yes, I'm sure. You know my mother . . . Besides, I have no idea what time I'll arrive. I'll call you from Chicago. Just you and Laura, okay?"

I was a nervous wreck all the next day. I couldn't concentrate or sleep. I couldn't talk on the phone or go anywhere. I was afraid to miss his call. I cleaned the apartment, changed Laura's clothes and mine several times, and I baked a sherry cake, his favorite. For a while I thought that he wouldn't call again, that he would get a cab at the airport and just show up at the door. When it had been almost twenty-four hours without hearing from him and it was Laura's bedtime, I decided to ask Kai's mother if she would be able to stay with Laura while I went to the airport. It was half past midnight when I finally got Paul's call. Gloria, a single woman from upstairs, ended up coming over. I drove carefully since I hardly ever ventured out in the dark. The airport was almost deserted. It didn't seem that any flight was expected. I was still walking around asking questions when I saw a small aircraft taxiing down the runway.

Paul was home. Just as simple as that. He was back. He had made it in one piece. We were among the lucky ones, after all. The general had been right all along—not a scratch on him.

Later, we hugged behind the closed door of the apartment and cried quietly in each other's arms. I could feel Paul's wet, warm, happy tears running down the back of my neck, the only time in my life I remember him crying. I turned on the hallway light and peeked in Laura's room. I thought we were being quiet, but she had awakened.

"Oh my god, she's standing up in her crib," Paul said. "She is so big!"

Oh my god, I thought, is he in for a surprise! Poor Laura was crying too, confused by what was happening. I picked her up and held her out to Paul, but she wouldn't go to her father's arms. He was simply a total stranger to her, no matter how many times I cooed, "He's your daddy, Laura. You want to give him a kiss?"

He seemed deliriously happy, and I know I was. His eyes were gleaming, and there was a rare, toothy smile on his face. When Laura finally quieted down and went back to sleep, we took a shower together. He had lost weight since I had seen him in Hawaii, but felt solid and real, stronger than in my dreams. I always liked that he was so tall and felt protected in his arms.

"Let's see, whose turn is it to get on top?" he asked, resuming our life as husband and wife as if we had made love the night before instead of almost five months earlier.

"I thought you were too tired," I teased.

"I'm wasted, but I don't think I can get to sleep now. I'm too wound up." The way I remember, it is that we stayed up all night. We made love twice and then tried again until *soldadito* was AWOL and I was raw and sore, contented, and at peace.

I don't know what time it was when the phone rang, but we didn't pick it up. Whoever was calling would know that either Paul had arrived home already, or that I was on my way to the airport to get him. Then he wanted to open some gifts; the jinx was over. We ate the sherry cake and drank Spanish brut.

The next day, starting first thing in the morning, our parents and friends came unannounced. Even neighbors I hardly knew stopped by because they heard the marine was home.

"I thought you didn't have any friends," he pretended to complain. The truth is that I really didn't know I had.

Laura was slow to warm up to him. She started waking up in the middle of the night again, which she hadn't done in months, and she was unusually clingy to me. She was a lot bigger than he had imagined. "Like a three—or four-year-old Vietnamese kid," he kept repeating.

"It's so scary to think that despite all the photos you sent, I wouldn't have recognized my own child."

We didn't throw a party nor had any other celebration. Paul insisted that we keep everything low-key since the news from Vietnam was so upsetting. The Tet Offensive had claimed over three thousand American lives already, and of course, many of his friends were still over there. Four men in his squadron had died, and one, Hugh Fanning, had been shot down over North Vietnam and remained MIA. He was Sylvia's husband, the woman with whom I took driving lessons.

Since the Tet Offensive, the demonstrations on campus had started up again. The students were noisier and more committed than a year earlier, no doubt fearing the draft as well. The women too had taken on a new role. We could hear them chanting,

"Girls say *yes* to guys who say *no*!"

"So much for coming home a hero," Paul would say.

He couldn't wait to get away from the university atmosphere and be back with his squadron. "This isn't like World War II, huh, Dad?" I heard him ask his father. *Abuelito* had to get in on it too, and he told us with his accustomed mirth that the Americans were finally going to find out what it was like to lose a war.

"Van a ver ellos lo que es perder una guerra."

With all the leave Paul had accumulated, there were six weeks before he had to report in California. His parents were disappointed that we would leave so soon. His father arranged for him to speak at the Rotary Club. This is the last newspaper clipping in his mother's album, "Rotary to Hear Viet Report":

> A Marine will give a slide-illustrated talk about his tour of duty in Vietnam at the Tuesday luncheon meeting of the Rotary Club. Capt. Paul Davidson was in Vietnam 13 months and flew 160 combat missions in support of the operations against the Communist (Vietcong) Insurgent Forces with the Marine Fighter-Attach Squadron-115. During the last five months, he was also the Civic Affairs Officer for the Marine Aircraft Group 13. As part of his duties, he aided in the building of schools and dispensaries and general cleanup of war-damaged villages. The program originally scheduled for Tuesday, a talk by Dr. Warren Hansen of Purdue University, has been postponed until a later date.

Laura stayed with my parents while Paul and I drove straight through to California in six days. It wasn't a sightseeing trip. We had to find a place to live and were eager to get settled. In a hotel lounge in Dallas, we saw President Johnson announcing on TV that he was halting the US bombing campaign over North Vietnam and would not run for a second term. Paul was elated, and although talking about the war made him sad in those days and not angry yet, he blurted out, making a fist,

"Serves him right, that son of a bitch! Now he's also a casualty of war."

On April 4, we had gone to see the movie studios in Los Angeles when we heard that Martin Luther King Jr. had been slain in Memphis. Little did we know that two months later, a few blocks from where we were standing, Robert Kennedy would also be gunned down. One of the worst years of our personal lives had just finished, but politically, one of the worst was just beginning for the good old US of A.

I was so angry anyway with the military establishment that I just wanted to be as far as possible from Camp Pendleton. We decided, after a lot of discussion, not to live on the base, particularly since base housing was in the middle of the California desert.

"For god's sake, Paul, haven't we been through enough? I won't stand living in another military compound." I insisted on a place closer to the seaside, as far away as possible from the base.

"Besides, it makes sense. We wouldn't have to move again if we decide to stay in California after you leave the Marine Corps."

"Are you kidding? You won't want to be so far away from your parents."

"You know what?" I said to him, exasperated, "I've had enough of parents and in-laws for a while."

Grandmother Davidson, always eager to get in the action, flew with Laura to Los Angeles as soon as we found an apartment in San Clemente, right across the highway from Rancho Santa Margarita, which would become President Nixon's western White House. We could almost see the Pacific from our roof terrace, and we definitely could feel its breezes and also the Santa Ana winds coming from the mountains, as we would soon find out.

Surely, there were some adjustment problems between Laura and her dad. At first she had a very hard time sharing her mommy with him, but eventually, she got used to having him around—that is, as long as I was in the house. Even if I left the room, she would start screaming and holding her breath. We should have asked the doctor or sought some kind of help. Instead, I just never left her alone with her father—a big mistake on my part. Soon, she was able to make herself vomit whenever I was out of her sight. I wasn't aware that children could vomit at will. I found out the hard way. Paul was very impatient with the whole situation.

"Damn, if she isn't a charmer, but she sure can be a pest. I think you've spoiled her rotten." Of course I was the one to be blamed if there were any problems with Laura's behavior.

"It's just a matter of time, be patient with her." But he'd get angry with me. As usual, I kept trying to create this picture-perfect family, especially then, with the daddy finally at home.

She woke up one Sunday morning while I was out on a quick errand and promptly tried vomiting, but lucky for us all, she couldn't do it on an empty stomach. Laura must have thought she had lost the knack because she never tried it again. I came in and her father was smiling, feeding her some hot cereal.

"Voilá." He grinned.

We were a happy family at last!

SPANISH DAUGHTER

I

On the evening of her mother's funeral, Inmaculada discovered that during her mother's lengthy illness, her father had been having an affair with one of her aunts.

Her mother's death, although expected, was in itself a traumatic experience. In an early-morning phone call, Inma's brother, who had been taking care of their mother in Madrid for the final few months, informed Inma of her passing. Inma had to put her feelings aside for the moment and go into action. If she hurried, she could still leave that same day. She needed to see if her mother-in-law could fly in from Indiana to Atlanta to take care of her two daughters, eight-year-old Laura and three-year-old Andrea. Paul could miss work for one day, but not more. Besides, he had never taken care of the girls on his own—patience had never been his strong suit—and Inma didn't feel comfortable leaving them with him.

"Thanks so much, Constance," Inma told her mother-in-law on the phone. "Yes, I know you were fond of my mother. You were really very good to her the last few years before she left for Spain." Inma could count on her mother-in-law, who thrived on feeling needed, to give her a hand.

"Don't worry about a thing, dear," she reassured Inma. "I'll call Paul with my flight time so he can pick me up at the airport."

"I purchased a ticket for a week's stay," Inma said. "I should be back for Laura's birthday, but if I need to remain in Madrid longer, the invitations and the magician have already been arranged. Just buy some prepared food at the supermarket. I was going to order the cake today."

"Don't fret, Inmaculada, dear. I'll take care of it. Just get yourself ready, and I'll call Paul when I have a reservation."

It often happened that way. Her in-laws came through when it mattered. They weren't there for the thoughtful little things on an everyday basis, but they were the most reliable in emergencies. For example, when Paul had arrived from Vietnam, Grandmother Constance had flown with little Laura to the West Coast, giving her mom and dad time to get reacquainted and a bit settled.

Inma's professors at the university were also understanding; she could make up the work later. Always a serious student, she hardly ever missed a class. After a ten-year hiatus in her studies, Inma was planning to finish her degree in record time. One more regular semester and one of summer school, and she would be a college graduate, something her own mother never accomplished but had always wanted for her daughter.

Andrea was too young to understand about the death. She had been with *Abuelita*, her Spanish grandmother, on a few occasions and had enjoyed drawing and playing bakery with her during the weeks she had stayed with them in Atlanta. But she knew Grandma Davidson much better and would be excited to see her. Laura cried, heartbroken, when her mother picked her up at school early and told her the sad news. Inma hadn't wanted Laura to get home and find out about *Abuelita* without her mother there to console her. This was the first time Laura lost someone. Now one of her grandmothers was gone, and she hadn't had a chance to say good-bye to her. From the time she was a baby, Laura had felt a tight bond with her maternal grandparents. She spoke Spanish with them and had traveled to Madrid the summer before to see her *Abuelita* one more time before she died, which everyone knew was imminent but didn't admit openly.

"Oh, Momma, I'm so sad. What is *Abuelito* going to do now?" Laura asked, rubbing her eyes with both fists.

"Don't you worry, sweetheart. He'll be fine. We'll ask him to visit us as soon as he is ready, and we'll pep him up." Inma knew that her father hadn't been too sad without his wife. She suspected that he was involved with some young student. Even before her mother left for Spain, he used to have one flirtation after another, practically under his wife's nose. Heaven knew what he had been up to during the last few months while *Abuelita* was dying in Madrid.

Always trying to be the concerned, thoughtful daughter, Inma didn't want to jump to conclusions and had kept her suspicions to herself. Paul didn't seem to like her parents as much as he used to, her father in particular, so she didn't want to give him any more ammunition by voicing her concerns. It worked out that Inma's and her father's flights were to arrive in New York at about the same time. They would meet at JFK, in the TWA international terminal, and fly together to Madrid. She dreaded the trip.

* * *

The trips to Spain were always stressful with all the required visits to relatives, the competition and tensions that had built up from years of distance. Her brother, in particular, and her cousins too, were specialists in one-upmanship. They took every opportunity to compare the United States with old Europe and were eager to criticize anything American. At least this time she could tell them she was finishing her degree and was planning to continue straight on to graduate school, to become a college professor like her father. The many times Inma's mother had reminded her that she had married too young without finishing her studies had finally made an impact, even if *Abuelita* would not be there to see her daughter graduate from college.

Once Inma was alone on the flight to New York City, she could concentrate on the reason for this trip and recognize that she felt sad and somewhat guilty. She would never see her mother alive again. Her thin, short frame with the head full of wavy reddish hair. Her fine features reflected now on little Andrea's face. Her beautiful, always well-kept hands, much like Inma's own. Her cool demeanor, which Inma hadn't mastered yet, although she had inherited her mother's resourcefulness. *Abuelita* had been so sick for so long, and it had been very painful to drag her from place to place trying to find a new experimental treatment that would buy her a few more months of life. Inma herself had taken her to Emory University Hospital, hoping they could find a cure for her damaged liver; and her mother had been, in fact, on a waiting list to be one of the first liver transplants. She would have been an excellent candidate because of her relatively young age and healthy heart and lungs. At least she had stopped suffering now, and Inma could start to grieve.

It was too late to kiss her one more time. Why was her mother's skin always cool to the touch? Too late to tell her how much she loved her, "Te quiero mucho, *Mamá*." So simple and so easy to think about it, and so hard to say when Inma's mother was still alive. Why hadn't Inma flown to visit her when she was admitted to the hospital in Madrid right after Christmas? After many hospitalizations, who could have known that this one would be the last?

She dreaded the trip for many reasons. Junior, her brother, would act self-righteous again, having been there for his mother to the very end. What did he understand about raising two children without much help? He seemed to forget that Inma didn't have a live-in maid to cook and take care of the children and another who came twice a week to do the heavy cleaning, like people in Spain still had. He wasn't aware that Inma didn't have a single relative anywhere near Atlanta, where she now lived. Her mother-in-law had to come from Indiana in case of an emergency, like this time. Paul's work was his life. He was a helpful husband around the house, but only with the usual male tasks: the lawn, the cars, the furnace. He couldn't be counted on to take care of the girls for a few days. He actually wasn't different from her brother in that respect.

Despite the confusion of the crowded walkways, the rows of escalators, the glare of the bright lights, and the loud announcements of flights arriving and leaving at JFK airport, Inma saw her father immediately. He was sitting at a table on a restaurant's mezzanine, looking for her among the crowd of travelers.

"*Papá*, how are you doing?" she asked him sadly as they gave each other a tight hug.

His back felt strong despite his slender appearance. He was dressed well with a professorial tweed jacket and a sweater underneath, his heavy coat folded over a chair. He didn't look like a grieving widower. Inma had also brought her heaviest winter coat, a shearling trimmed with curly lamb's wool, her mother's last gift to her. Madrid could be very cold in the winter months, often damp and gray with a chilling wind coming from the mountains. She wondered if she looked like a grieving daughter herself.

"You may not believe it, but I'm so overcome that I can hardly speak" were her father's first words.

He often had a way of knowing what Inma was thinking. No, she didn't believe him, but she was glad that he didn't want to speak. She was emotionally exhausted, and the thought of listening to him during the overnight flight to Madrid was downright frightful. Being solemn was one side of him; the other was a chatterbox who could take days to tell a story. He lived up to his Gemini sign without a doubt. He loved to repeat his ideas until Inma, exhausted, would agree with him.

"Tienes razón, Papá." And even then he could go on for hours around and around the same arguments.

Since they had made the reservations that very day, their seats were not together. The airline hostess offered to find two side-by-side seats as soon as the plane doors were closed, but Inma assured her that it wasn't necessary, that her father wanted to be in the smoking section, and they hoped to sleep anyway. Inma really doubted that she would be able to sleep, but at least she could keep her eyes closed and pretend. She just wanted to think and rest. Later, when she sat up to pick at her dinner, she could see her father, a few rows in back of her, flirting with the flight attendant. Amazing how his English improved when he had to make himself understood by a young woman. Inma dozed on and off until she heard the warnings for landing and felt the bumps of the runway.

*　*　*

Barajas airport was darker and quieter than usual, and it smelled of stale tobacco. Overseas flights always arrived early in the morning, before the airport shops were open, without the employees walking about, talking loudly and smoking everywhere. This time it was still dark outside and very cold, quite a contrast from the summer months full of tourists. Inma had flown into Madrid in the winter once before for her wedding some ten years earlier, but she hadn't noticed the austerity of the place then.

"That's odd. Junior isn't here," she said to her father as they started walking side by side to the customs area.

He didn't bother to answer. Apparently, he didn't think it was odd that his wife's death would intensify the estrangement between his son and him. Relations had been civil up to that point, but only to keep up appearances in front of the sick mother.

Inma called her brother's home. The maid answered, obviously awakened by the call that early in the morning.

"Puri, I'm sorry, I didn't mean to wake you. I just didn't want to leave the airport if my brother was on his way to pick us up." Inma was still surprised that no one had come to meet them. Junior got on the line without trying to hide how sleepy he was.

"As you can imagine, we only had a few hours' sleep, with all the arrangements," Junior said, not wasting any time with pleasantries.

"I don't think we slept at all," Inma answered, already on the defensive. "And we're jet-lagged. It's like three o'clock in the morning for us." The competition had started.

"The baby was up all night, she could feel that something was wrong." Junior was not going to give up so soon. "There will be a viewing at eleven, and the burial is at one." As usual, Junior thought he had everything under control.

Inma knew that traditionally in Spain, perhaps from an old Jewish custom, the funeral takes place within twenty-four hours; thus, people are not usually embalmed. She wondered whether her brother would have waited if she and their father hadn't been able to make the first plane to Madrid. It's not like they lived in New York and could catch a direct flight at a moment's notice.

"Claro que no" (Of course not), her father responded when Inma shared her concerns with him. They would have gone ahead with the funeral without them.

Junior's house was not much friendlier than the phone call. The family was up by the time Inma and her father arrived from the airport by cab, but hardly hiding how tired they were and how horrible the last few weeks had been.

"The baby is so adorable," Inma said, missing her own daughters already. Pilucha, with big dark eyes and shiny black hair, looked very different from her American cousins with their lighter hair and complexion.

Inma's sister-in-law was in the bathroom getting ready. By the time the travelers opened their bags, showered, and got dressed, people had started arriving. The phone hadn't stopped ringing since they walked in. Some of the relatives were driving from Valencia, having started the drive early to make it on time. The competition for the most-suffering-one was in full swing by the time they all left for the hospital where the funeral was to begin.

Not all of *Abuelita's* six siblings could make it. The youngest sister, who lived in France, was ill with breast cancer. Two of the brothers were the first to arrive; only one had brought his wife, and the remaining brother and his wife were not there either. Each of the relatives gave a cursory greeting to the widower, who had never gotten along well with his wife's family. The brothers were still tall and handsome with the same wavy hair as Inma's mother, their older sister. It upset Inma that they barely recognized her.

"Have I changed that much? Where are Uncle Alberto and Aunt Amparo? Aren't they coming?" Inma had asked each uncle and aunt as they arrived at Junior's house.

Inma hadn't seen most of them but once or twice since her wedding over ten years ago, and then just for short visits. Only Aunt Amparo had always kept in touch and, at one point, was even planning to go to the States to visit Inma's parents there. That's why it was so odd that Aunt Amparo and Uncle Alberto hadn't come. They usually spent some time with her parents during their summers in Spain. Inma thought that perhaps her aunt was sick as well. She would inquire again later.

In what seemed to Inma like an odd arrangement, the basement of the hospital served as a funeral parlor. Just getting into the building was a complicated event because none other than General Francisco Franco was also hospitalized there at the same time; thus, security was extremely tight around the entire Barrio de Salamanca neighborhood. All kinds of government officials stopped by daily to pay their respects, thinking for many weeks that the old dictator was about to die. Barricades, police cars with flashing lights, and journalists from different parts of the world were buzzing about, creating quite a commotion.

Two other families were burying their loved ones that morning. Each casket was laid in a separate cubicle overflowing with their respective flower arrangements. All the families gathered together in a central area discussing the imminent death of the country's head of state. The relatives of a young man who had died in a motorcycle accident were almost joking and repeating,

"Why couldn't that old goat Franco have died instead?"

Inma had asked to see her mother one last time, and her two uncles offered to accompany her into the private cubicle. Her father said that he didn't want to remember his wife that way. Inma's mother was in the back corner. A simple white wreath lay on the closed part of the casket. Without even noticing it fully, she read on the inscription, "Tu hijo que no te olvida." Evidently, her son didn't forget, but Inma and her father had not thought about flowers. Inma was distraught that her brother had not simply inscribed it in the plural—"*tus hijos*"—to include her, even if he wanted to exclude their father at a time like that. For a moment, instead of feeling sadness at the sight of her mother's body, Inma felt anger at her brother and father. As far as she was concerned, they were both at fault for bickering, and she hated being caught in the middle.

Her mother's face looked dark and dry, almost a bronze color. Her eyes, such a beautiful hazel shade, were not fully closed, revealing a yellow opaque substance. The cotton balls inside her nostrils protruded onto her lips, which were even darker than her skin. Her mouth had an awkward grimace, ending all hope that she had died peacefully. She was tiny—much, much thinner than Inma had ever seen her. Her beautiful hands had dried up into two hooks of bunched fingers. Her hair lacked its habitual shine, and gray roots showed all around her forehead. When Inma touched her head, it felt like straw.

Finally, tears flooded Inma's face; uncontrollable, warm, quiet tears fell onto her mother's body as she gave her a farewell kiss. Inma became aware of her arms being pulled on either side as her uncles led her out into the central hall. The rest of the morning, Inma felt as if she had walked into someone's nightmare and wanted to wake up to be in her own dream, someplace familiar. The next time she looked toward the corner, her mother's casket was gone and people were filing out, getting into taxis and following the black hearse. Inma didn't know where her brother or father was. She found herself sitting stiffly between her two uncles in the back of a taxicab.

The drive to the San Isidro y Santos Justo y Pastor cemetery was cold and long. Traffic was almost at a standstill during the lunch rush hour, even away from the congestion of the hospital. The trees past Plaza de Atocha were bald and tall. Not a bit of color was left on the boulevards heading toward the outskirts of the city. A cloudy, gray morning was turning into a misty, freezing afternoon. At the walled main entrance to the cemetery, the flower stalls were still open. Inma thought of asking the taxi driver to stop, but she hadn't changed money yet and decided that she would come back by herself another day, before returning to the States, and bring her own flowers.

Inma had never been inside the walls of the cemetery. She remembered seeing it only from the outside when she used to go, as a little girl, with her parents and her brother to the Casa de Campo for a picnic or to ride her bike. As with many parts of Madrid, the cemetery was undergoing a major renovation, and construction equipment was strewn on both sides of the road. Rows and rows of walls were being built, with their neatly empty niches, waiting for tenants. There didn't seem to be any more room underground for burials. One had to go farther out of the city, to the Almudena cemetery, she was told, to find that kind of space available.

The cars stopped at the old entrance framed by tall wrought-iron gates. Everyone walked in silence behind the gurney that carried the casket. This old part of the cemetery was full of family mausoleums with statues of angels, Madonnas, saints, the effigies of famous people. Although several monuments had beautiful, fresh arrangements on them, it smelled of putrid flowers. Cats scurried about, upset at being disturbed. One or two solitary people stood by a tomb or kneeled quietly by the headstone of a deceased relative.

"They should have laid her to rest in Valencia, where she was born," Inma heard her uncles whisper to each other. "This place is so huge and foreboding."

Inma felt numb and didn't comment. Nothing could change the fact that her mother was dead now. Did it really matter where she was buried? It was the first time Inma had to bury someone and see a cemetery this intimately. When her grandparents died, she was too little to attend the funeral, and her cousin Luisita passed away after Inma was already living in the States.

As the group entered a newer area with smaller statues and more walls like the ones being built out front, Inma was trying to pay attention to all the twists and turns so she would be able to come back by herself. Some families stood nearby praying in hushed tones. Around a bend in a newer section, there were two workmen standing and waiting, each holding a wheelbarrow full of fresh cement.

Inma's family came to a stop, and the gurney inched up to the top row of the wall, where a scaffold had been set up in front of an open niche. The priest, who had joined them at the cemetery gates, said a few prayers in Latin. Inma stared at her brother and his wife standing in front of her in the semicircle. Her father was at the other side with some of his academic friends. Inma was still shaking, supported by her two uncles. She felt frozen inside all the way to her bones. As soon as the casket disappeared into the wall, the two workers climbed onto the scaffold and began plastering the niche closed with perfunctory efficiency. Soon after, the people started to disperse as if they were in a hurry to disappear. Someone she didn't recognize asked Inmaculada how her daughters and husband were. "Fine, fine, everyone is doing well." Her tongue felt thick, as if she were waking up after a long sleep.

"Will you have enough time to come to Valencia later this week?" a cousin asked, guiding her toward the cemetery entrance.

"No, no, not this time, but I'll visit again soon, I promise. Is anything wrong with Aunt Amparo and Uncle Alberto? How come they haven't made it to my mother's funeral?" Without realizing it, Inma was taking the family's attendance roll, very much like her mother would have done.

"That's right, Inmaculada, they are not feeling well. They send their condolences. You know how much Uncle Alberto loved your mother."

"I know, I know, that's why it's so strange." She noticed that her family was calling her by her full first name, *Inmaculada,* which used to be reserved for her mother, and not the shorter version, *Inma.* She had moved up in the hierarchy, even if in her heart, she would always be her mother's daughter.

*   *   *

Back in her brother's house, lunch was prepared for the relatives who had come from out of town. Puri had made some hearty soup and empanadas, something quick so they could get back to Valencia on the same day. Except for a light breakfast, Inmaculada and her father hadn't eaten since dinner on the plane in what felt like ages ago. Nevertheless, her father excused himself to take a nap in his old study, which now was the family room. Inma couldn't wait to get some sleep herself, but stayed up until the last family members left saying, "Adiós, adiós, Inmaculada, ven a vernos pronto con tus niñas, ¿eh?" Yes, Inma promised, she would come back with her daughters and visit them soon.

Inma went to get some rest in her old room, the baby's room now. Pilucha had been moved with her crib into her parents' bedroom. Despite the new decor, Inma recognized the daybed that used to be in the spare room, which had become Puri's. She lay down thinking she'd sleep the rest of the day, but to her own amazement, she felt completely awake. She could smell her mother's scent on the pillow—the lavender mixed with the citrus of her cologne. She had probably used this room too before she left for the hospital. It was reassuring to know that *Abuelita* had a chance to meet little Pilucha even if she had never seen her three granddaughters together, as she had hoped. The scenes of the day in the hospital, the ride to the cemetery, and the burial kept replaying in Inma's head. She decided to get up for a glass of water to take a sleeping pill even if it meant she would sleep the rest of the day.

Her sister-in-law was sitting in the living room, dozing off.

"Where's Junior?" Inma asked, trying to be friendly.

"He went to the office. He's so far behind with all that's been happening the last few weeks. Come and sit for a minute," Clara said, tapping the sofa. "There is something you should know." Inma didn't know her sister-in-law well. Whenever she came to visit, Clara was busy working late, and they seldom connected. Perhaps that's why Inma didn't tell her that she just wanted to get a drink of water and go back to bed.

"I heard you asking your uncles about your Aunt Amparo," Clara began.

"Yes, isn't it odd that she didn't come? What's going on?" Inma feared another untimely illness.

"*Escucha*, listen here. Your father has been having an affair with your Aunt Amparo for the last couple of years," Clara blurted out.

Inma was stunned. "Are you nuts? What are you saying?" If she could only rewind and go back to bed, she would never have to find out. But Clara was on a mission and couldn't be stopped now.

"It started two summers ago. You remember how Uncle Alberto and Aunt Amparo always made it a point to visit your parents in Madrid."

"I know, I know, I've even seen the photos. But are you sure?" Inma was still trying to set back the clock.

"Your mother was not feeling well at all, and her brother Alberto would stay with her, keeping her company while your dad and Amparo went to the Prado Museum or to some exhibit," Clara continued with certain malice. "You know how much he likes to show off his superior intellect. It all started that way, innocently enough. You know how charming your father can be when he wants to—"

"How did you find out about it?" Inma interrupted, unready yet to believe her.

"In fact, last summer, Aunt Amparo herself contacted Junior and me, trying to enlist our help. She was ready to leave Uncle Alberto and move to the United States to be with your father, pretending that she was going to take care of your poor mother. Your brother showed her the door immediately, I hope you know."

Inma listened in complete silence.

"Aunt Amparo feared that Uncle Alberto would find out. She had become terrified of him. By then the entire family was aware of their relationship. They either had seen it themselves or some relative had informed them."

Just as Clara was doing just then, thought Inma.

"I can't believe I didn't realize what my dad was up to," she said, thinking out loud now, trying to put two and two together. "No wonder my mother left my father behind and wouldn't stay in the States, saying she wanted to die in her home country. She probably knew. Did she ever let on to you?"

"No, she never said anything, but while she was at the hospital, she never asked for Amparo either. I think she knew." The more Clara spoke, the worse the entire affair became.

"Let me tell you how it all came unraveled—"

"No, por favor, Clara, ya es bastante." That was enough. Inma would speak to her father and get to the bottom of it later. She couldn't bear to hear her sister-in-law's delight in her father's failings any longer. She knew very well that Clara had never cared for him.

The sleeping pill didn't take effect for a long time. Inma tried to lie quietly in her old room with her eyes closed, but nothing was the same anymore, not the house where she had grown up nor her family. She found herself thinking obsessively about her dad and her aunt Amparo. Instead of feeling sad because her mother had died, she was furious at her father's betrayal. She couldn't call Paul and share this with him; he would be even angrier than she was. At one point during the evening, Inma thought she could hear her brother and dad arguing, but she didn't fully wake up. She slept until the next morning, missing dinner.

When she woke up the second day in Madrid, she felt as if she had been there a week. It was like a hangover. She looked at herself in the tiny mirror of her traveling case and thought she seemed ten years older. Maybe the whole thing had been a dream and only her mother's funeral was true. She felt she could deal with her mother's death better than with the affair. But as soon as she stepped out of the bathroom, her brother was there to bring her back to reality.

"I hear that Clara brought you up-to-date!" Junior would do anything to have her team up with him against their old man. But luckily, he was rushing out the door and nothing else was said.

*   *   *

Inma needed to clear her head. She told Puri that she wouldn't be in to eat lunch. She had decided to spend as little time as possible at her brother's house. She would rather visit the relatives who lived in Madrid. She wanted to see her favorite, Aunt Elena, and some of the cousins she had barely spoken to the day before. And she could take advantage of any time left to buy some books on her graduate school reading list. She would get some Spanish fairy tales she had promised the girls and maybe a matching outfit for the two of them, even though Laura hated when her mother, in the old Spanish way, dressed her up like her little sister. She also needed to purchase a baby gift for Pilucha. Inma felt bad that she wasn't paying much attention to her.

Aunt Elena, Inma's godmother, confirmed that what Clara had told her was true and added a few details of her own: "Aunt Amparo had even taken some short trips with your parents."

"Of course, I've seen the photos." Inma could remember Aunt Amparo's beautiful round face. Although there wasn't much age difference, with her rosy cheeks and perfect smile, she looked a lot younger than Inma's mother. There was one picture taken in the Botanical Gardens in Valencia that showed her leaning on a tree as if she were a movie star. Now Inma knew who she was posing for.

Inma's father didn't want to spend much time around the house either. He had legal matters to attend to and needed to speak with his publisher. Then he called to say that he would stay a couple of days at El Escorial, their place in the mountains outside Madrid. He wanted to check out the apartment while he was in Spain.

Later that week, on a sunny, cold morning, Inma took a taxi and went back to the cemetery. She stopped at the entrance and bought a big bouquet of pink carnations with baby's breath. The flower vendor asked her, "¿Son para su madre? La acompaño en el sentimiento."

Inma nodded her head up and down. She was moved to tears to think that a complete stranger, who saw so many people getting flowers every day, would give her condolences. It was an epiphany for her. Do people who have lost their mother look different? Inmaculada felt a newness in her, a strong realization of being somehow alone but at the same time very much connected. She promised herself that she would bring Laura and Andrea to put flowers by *Abuelita's* grave as soon as they were able to make the trip together.

Although the sun seemed to make everything look different from just a few days ago, Inma found her way through the labyrinth of pathways and started to recognize the areas she had walked by with her relatives. The workers were busy at the construction site; they must have been eating lunch the time before. The snow-covered mountains, which had been hidden by the clouds the day of the burial, could be seen in the distance; they looked almost blue. Only the smell of the forgotten flowers was the same. Her mother's resting place had changed its appearance too. The scaffolding had been removed, the slab of concrete looked dry, and at each side there were two flower holders, which Inma had not noticed earlier. She wasn't sure how to reach up that high until she saw a folded ladder standing in a corner. Inma agreed with her uncles then; why wasn't her mother buried in Valencia with her own side of the family instead of being alone among strangers in this cemetery?

As she had promised, Inma went to say good-bye to Aunt Elena on the last evening before leaving Madrid.

"Ni una palabra sobre la tía Amparo, ¿eh?" They agreed not to dwell on Aunt Amparo and Inma's father any longer, but it was hard not to.

"Guess who stopped by this evening? You just missed her." Inma wasn't sure she could handle any more surprises. "Your cousin Amparín, Amparo's daughter."

Inma hardly remembered her. All these cousins had grown up since she and her parents moved to the United States. She had run into Amparín's older brother years ago during a quick trip to Valencia, but she wouldn't have recognized her cousin if she had passed her in the street (as she probably had).

Maybe it was a good thing she hadn't seen her cousin. She wouldn't know what to tell her. She had been so submerged in her own pain that she hadn't realized she wasn't the only one dealing with their parents' mistakes.

"Amparín left something for you. She's been suffering too, with it all . . . She has been studying in Madrid for a year now." Inma didn't know exactly what to say. But Aunt Elena was right; the entire family was affected by the stupid affair. It was a small package, probably a book, although it felt lighter. Perhaps something for the girls?

*   *   *

Inmaculada was determined to speak to her father on the return trip to the States, even if she had to sit in the smoking section and smell like a chimney by the end of the flight. He had obviously been avoiding her all this past week. They took a taxi together and rode to the airport in silence. He was the first to approach the subject.

"We need to talk. Heaven only knows what your brother has been telling you. He never misses an opportunity for family discord."

"I'm ready whenever you stop hiding from me," Inma replied.

Barajas was much busier in the middle of the day than on the morning they had arrived. The cafeterias were overflowing with people drinking their last cups of Spanish coffee and smoking. The duty-free shops had lines of shoppers waiting to spend their last pesetas.

Being at the airport made Inma think of her family back home. Inma couldn't wait to see the girls and talk with Paul. It sure felt longer than a week since she had left them. She was aware that her home was not in Madrid any longer. But she had lived in Atlanta only a little over a year. Was that home? Perhaps home was people—her husband and daughters—and not a place anymore. The flight was delayed. How she hoped she wouldn't arrive late for her connection in New York! She didn't want to miss Laura's birthday nor spend another night away from home.

During the flight, the hostesses had already cleared away the lunch trays, but Inma's father hadn't yet opened up to her.

"Bueno, Papá, a ver qué me cuentas," Inma urged her father to tell her what he had in mind.

"Inmaculada," he began, "you have always been an understanding daughter." Inma didn't acknowledge the compliment.

"You are the only one who witnessed how I took care of your mother for many years. As you know, she'd been ill ever since you were young." He was gaining confidence; nothing would stop him now.

He went back to the years in Valencia when Inma and her brother were little children. How hard he had to work, teaching world history at the university and several other schools to make ends meet. How he went from place to place on his motorcycle and arrived home when his children were already in bed. He still found time to write until two or three in the morning, hoping to publish some essays in the local press. How stifled he felt under Franco's dictatorship those first years after the Spanish Civil War, having fought for the opposition on the Republican front. What it was like to be afraid that anyone could denounce him to the authorities, accusing him of being a liberal. One could be imprisoned simply for speaking the regional languages, as he made sure to do at home, despite his wife's admonitions. How careful he needed to be in the classroom and in his writing. How strict the government censorship was in every aspect of his life!

Inmaculada had heard this story many times before, but she wasn't going to interrupt her father. His exculpatory monologue went on. How he applied and won the first open position available at the university in Madrid, even though it wasn't in his field. How his family had to help him buy their first home in the capital, the same one that Junior had taken over in the last few years, where he didn't have a comfortable place to sleep now. How his wife didn't want to move to Madrid and complained incessantly about her health and not living in Valencia, her hometown.

The movie had started on the overhead screen, and Aunt Amparo's name hadn't been mentioned yet. Inma knew how thorough her father could be. He was well into it now. How Inma and her brother had attended the best schools on a scholarship, thanks to his position at the university. How he started to publish but still felt confined, stifled, in Spain. How he jumped at the chance to go to the States with the Fulbright Program during the 1960s. How proud he was to be able to take his family and open their lives to all kinds of opportunities. Inmaculada remembered that feeling too, and once she started college in the States, she knew it would be impossible for her to return to Franco's Spain.

Her father acknowledged that Inma was the only one who seemed to appreciate all that he had done for them. No sooner had they settled in the new country than his wife went from missing Valencia to missing Madrid and refused to learn English or to drive. That's not how Inma remembered it. Her mother had understood more English than she let on, and her dad was resentful of it and didn't let her speak up. As for driving, Junior had always been the designated driver, and not even Inma was given a chance to do it. She had to learn years later at a military base, when she was already expecting her first child.

Of course, according to her father, Junior had contributed to the disintegration of their family by moving back to Madrid alone, which made his mother miss her only son terribly. Inma was well aware of who had been her mother's favorite; she didn't need reminding now.

After Inma had married so young and moved away, there he was providing for all his wife's needs: taking her to doctors, doing all those errands for her, driving her everywhere . . . At this point, Inma couldn't keep quiet any longer. "Just like my mother always took care of all your meals, your washing, your clean house." Now it was his turn to ignore her and point out that for many years he had felt underappreciated, unloved, and misunderstood by his wife.

Hearing her father deconstruct his marriage this way was more painful than Inma could have imagined. More distressing, perhaps, than not knowing the reasons why her father had betrayed her mother. If she could only stop him now. With barely a pause, he finally reached the point. "The rest, as they say, is history. Amparo was a breath of fresh air. She thought I was the most intelligent man she had ever met. She couldn't learn fast enough. She brought me joy." Yes, Inma thought, but she is married as were you, and she is your sister-in-law.

"In case you are thinking that she is my sister-in-law, let me tell you how it all came to an end. Poor Amparo has suffered greatly." Inma had not considered feeling sorry for her aunt, but knowing her father as she did made her think of how her aunt, too was a victim.

Aunt Amparo had rented a post-office box where she had received the mail from her paramour and sent her letters to him at the university's address. She had confided only in her sister Marlena, a young widow. "Do you remember meeting her? She is just gorgeous." Inma's father always described women by their looks. "By far the prettier of the two."

"No, I'm positive I never met her. I'm not even sure I knew that Aunt Amparo had a sister." Inma was not in an expansive mood.

"Well, Marlena betrayed her own sister. She told Uncle Alberto, and one day last fall, the two of them were hiding when Amparo arrived to pick up her mail. They caught her flagrante delicto. Imagine, her own sister! Except for her daughter, everyone turned against Amparo. I have no idea how she is doing now."

Inma felt exhausted by this family melodrama. She had heard from Aunt Elena that Amparo had continued to live in the same house with Uncle Alberto, but in separate bedrooms, in some sort of semi captivity, Bluebeard style, since Amparo was no longer allowed to go anywhere by herself. For a moment, she considered telling this to her dad, along with the fact that Amparín had stopped by to see her, but thought better of it. She had already begun feeling bad for her aunt and for her cousin, who was also caught in this predicament. She had something to hide too; she had seen her father's letters to Amparo in the package that Amparín had brought for her, and she certainly had no intention of letting him know that either.

The flight back to the States is always an hour longer than going to Europe, something to do with the headwinds. This time it seemed longer than ever. The movie hadn't finished by the time Inma's father got up to go to the lavatory, and something fell out of the pocket of his tweed jacket. Under other circumstances, Inma might not have opened the fancy velvet box, but she did this time. Inside was a gold bracelet, almost identical to the one her mother had worn and from the same Madrid jewelry store, she was sure. What was going on? For whom was this bracelet intended? What was her dad up to now?

"Toma, Papá, se te ha caído algo." When he came back to his seat, Inma pointed out to her dad that he had dropped something. Almost proudly, he smiled with that squirrelly, sneaky look she was familiar with. She didn't find it funny or endearing anymore.

"¿Quieres que te cuente otra historia?" he asked her coyly.

Inma was sure that she didn't want to hear another story from him at that point.

*   *   *

When Inma arrived in Atlanta, Paul was pacing impatiently, waiting for her at the airport.

"What's with you? You look awful" were his first words.

"What do you think, that it was a pleasure trip?" How could he forget that coming back was always hard? They called it reentry, the military term used when the men came back from Vietnam. It's the going from one culture to another: different languages, different families, different problems. And this time was no exception.

"Everything is fine here. My mother has been great. The girls were good—excellent, I'd say. They bought you some flowers. Andrea has missed you the most, but she wanted to see the magic act. She's very excited about the birthday party, and Laura said she could stay. You'll be proud of her, she's been a good big sister, better than ever."

Inma's mind was still back in the plane, mulling over her father's revelations. It was a comfortable feeling getting back to the girls' squabbles and daily trivia.

"Wait until I tell you what's been going on with my family in Spain," Inma said as they walked to the car.

During the long drive on the interstate, which in typical Atlanta fashion was congested and slow, through the neighborhood streets and into the driveway, where they sat for a few minutes, Inma talked nonstop about her dad and Aunt Amparo. Paul listened intensely, but he didn't seem surprised.

"Your dad has always been an asshole, I say." Paul was usually quick to judge.

"It isn't that simple, Paul. It never is. Let's go inside, and do me a favor . . . don't tell your mother about this yet, okay?"

The screams "Momma's home! Momma's home!" and the sight of a lovely bouquet of early tulips on the foyer table brought Inma back to her sweet family. Mr. Nation, Laura's social studies teacher, who was also known for his magic shows, had already arrived and was setting up in the living room. Laura was proud to have him in her house.

"The best student in the class, I can tell you before anyone else gets here." Both Inma and Paul were used to hearing such accolades from Laura's teachers.

"*Whayou* bring me, Momma?" and a tight hug around her mother's legs were Andrea's welcome home. Inma noticed that her curly blond pigtails were more unruly than usual. She looked a tad older too in a fancy party dress that Inma had bought her earlier just for the occasion.

"They were two little angels, Inmaculada, dear. You should be very proud of them." Constance's praise had a way of turning into commands.

"Thanks so much, Grandma, it looks as if you guys got along famously." Inma realized that she had forgotten to buy something for her mother-in-law. She would have to give her some of the Spanish soap and cologne she had bought at the airport; Inma still preferred using them after more than ten years of living in the States.

The table was laid with paper plates; the matching decorations and party balloons were all set up in the dining room. The food was waiting in the kitchen, neatly covered. A big tray with colorful cupcakes, each with a candle in the middle, sat on the counter.

"Momma, we decided to make cupcakes instead of ordering a cake. Aren't they cute?" Laura seemed very pleased with her party arrangements.

"I helped with the *fosting*, Momma," Andrea chirped in.

When the children started arriving, Inma went upstairs to the bedroom to shower and unpack. This was home. Just looking at their cozy bedroom made her realize how much she had missed it in only a week. The curtains were not drawn yet, and she could see the tall pines waving in the breeze. She opened the door to the small deck just to smell the dry needles and feel the air. She could hear the children downstairs giggling and screaming. They had probably opened the patio doors. The bed looked inviting with the pillows neatly arranged. That's an advantage of being married to an ex-marine, Inma thought; Paul sure can make a perfect bed.

After taking a shower and getting dressed, Inma felt the weight of her trip again. Jet lag always hit her worse coming back than going over, the opposite of most people. She planned to simply peek at the birthday girl and her party and come back up to bed early. Constance and Paul were doing a fine job running things. They could finish the evening without her help. She was sure they'd understand.

She heard the phone ringing in the family room, but no one else seemed to. The party probably was drowning the sound.

Inma ran to answer it. "Hello?"

"Hi, Inmaculada. Is Constance there?" It was her father-in-law.

"Yes, sure. I'll get her. She's with the children at the birthday party."

"Don't bother her then. Ask her to call me when it's over." Inma was silent for a moment.

"Inmaculada, dear. Are you all right?" he asked.

"Well, you do know that my mother passed away, don't you? Since you haven't said anything about it." It was his turn to be quiet.

"Of course I know," he said after a pause. "I've written you a note. Haven't you received it?" She hadn't looked at her mail yet.

Inmaculada couldn't tell why it upset her so much that her father-in-law would not say anything about her mother on the phone even if he had written her a note. It had to be one of those cultural differences that always tripped her up. Was she overly sensitive, or were the others damn Yankees without feelings? Families could be equally strange on both sides of the Atlantic. Paul came into the room, saying that he thought he'd heard the phone ring.

"Yes, it was your dad. Can you believe that he didn't say anything about my mom?"

"You need to check your mail. I think he sent a note," Paul quickly retorted.

"Paul, you're just like them. It's so odd and so cold. Don't you understand? Even if he wrote a note, don't you think he could have said something when I answered the phone?"

"Inma, listen. Let me see if I got this straight. Your brother completely ignores you, but that's okay. Your father has been screwing around with your aunt while your mother was dying, and you understand. But you are mad at my dad because he didn't say something you wanted to hear. And we are odd or cold or whatever you say and you are the victim, right?" By the time he got it all out, Paul was screaming, full of anger.

"Please don't scream at me, not tonight, with Laura's party going on and your mother here. It's not that big a thing, I guess." Inma wanted peace in her family above all else. Maybe Paul was right and she was too sensitive.

By the time all the party guests had been picked up to go home and the gifts from Spain were opened, Inma was exhausted and excused herself to go up to bed. Paul didn't come up with her. A curt "good night, get some rest" were his only words.

Inma was crying quietly as the coolness of the pillow and sheets caressed her body. Sleep came quickly, taking her away to a much-needed rest. No matter how curious Inma was, the reading of her father's letters would have to wait for another day.

II

1 de septiembre 1973

Mi querida Amparo,

    I was already very nervous thinking that something had happened and you were not going to be able to write. It has been almost three weeks since we left Madrid, and I have missed you terribly. Mamá has not been feeling well from the time we arrived.

    A couple of things about your letter writing. Por favor, do not take it wrong, it is just to make things easier (who knows if these letters will be famous someday). Write "Professor" before my name. The secretary distributes all the mail, and I do not want her to get suspicious. She seems like a big gossiper; I see her chatting on the phone or with her assistant all the time. Do not buy airmail paper, por favor. It is not necessary, and it is very hard to read since you used both sides (I do like it that you wrote a long letter). In particular, the envelopes should not be airmail paper, or the secretary will be able to actually read the letter. You will need to write with big red letters (and clearly) on the outside that it is AIRMAIL, in addition to using the airmail stamp, of course. Have it weighed one time if you are not sure, but it should be fine. I guess you are an old-fashioned girl and you do not know these things.

Not so old-fashioned, though, since you have been able to rent the post-office box, and you are not afraid of the consequences of writing to your brother-in-law. In fact, one of the biggest surprises of our relationship for me has been how daring and exciting you are. I could not ask for more.

I think about you constantly, obsessively. We have several pictures of you in the living room (it is better this way. Mamá will think that I have nothing to hide), so I can look at your beautiful face whenever I want. I have not put any pictures out in my office, however. I have no idea who cleans it, but just in case. Besides, in this country, the students are coming constantly to our offices. Can you imagine? They are very spoiled, really. Other than to write your letters, I do not plan to be here at all. I never have. I do all the writing at home, on the dining room table, in fact. I have to give credit to Mamá who does not mind being quiet while I work and is agreeable to serving our meals at the kitchen table.

I have to run home now. I need to take Mamá to the grocery store. A Spanish colleague is coming for lunch, and she insists on making him a paella. I told her that he is from Sevilla, what does he know about paellas? But she insists; she can be very stubborn.

Be very careful and discreet. If we do this right, these letters can give us a lot of pleasure and be very little trouble. Do you not agree?

Siempre tuyo,
Juan José

7 de septiembre 1973

Queridísima Amparo,
Mamá is not feeling well. We have been running around seeing doctors without a stop. They think she should have a liver biopsy in Chicago as soon as possible. It is so hard for me to understand all this terminology. They speak as if they have chewing gum in their mouths (and sometimes they do), and then the technical language is just devilish. I do not like doctors

even in Spain. Thank goodness that Constance, my consuegra, has offered to take her to some doctors' visits. She loves being occupied. Who knows how those two understand each other, neither one speaks one word of the other's language.

I have been waiting for another letter from you all this week, but since it did not arrive, I decided to write to you first. It is a big relief for me to be able to communicate with you. You are the only person who understands what I am going through. My children are just waiting to judge me. If they think they could take better care of their mother, why do they not do it for a while and see how they like it? It is not an easy task.

Do not tell anyone about our correspondence, ¿sí? Not even your sister. I know you think she is a sweet woman, but it is better not to trust anyone. Did I ever tell you that Marlena is not nearly as beautiful as you are? Even so, I do not understand why she never married again. Imagine how jealous she would be if she knew that you were my paramour! I think she always looked at me with her roving eyes.

How are things at your home? Can you find enough time alone there to write? If you had some outside interests, it would be easier to leave the house and write in peace. You could go to a library to read. Find Pepita Jiménez by Juan Valera, and you will see what I mean by the pleasure of letter writing. He is a master.

Tu fiel,
Juan José

15 de septiembre 1973

Querida Amparito,

Gracias, gracias, gracias for your wonderful letter. It is amazing how a woman like you, without an education, can write with so much feeling. There has to be a reason why you and I have found each other this way. You make me extremely happy. You see how much easier it is to write on regular paper? The envelope is almost perfect as well. Just be careful to write the address a bit lower so that the mail seal does not cover it. Also, you do not need the return address. I notice that you only used your initials (very clever you are!), but it seems to me that a lost letter can do less harm than a letter in the wrong hands.

It saddens me immensely what you tell me about Alberto; he is a true *moro*, a barbarian. You know I am not fond of any of the brothers. They can be handsome, as you and Mamá say, but they have no soul (and all that hair makes their heads look too big). I wonder sometimes what they have inside their heads. The women in the family . . . that is another story! You remember how good-looking Mamá used to be. I do feel awful seeing her deteriorating and shrinking away like she is. She used to have the most beautiful head of hair, and now it is dull and dry, and she insists on wearing it short, when she knows how I love long hair. Forgive me if it upsets you when I write about my wife. You are my only consolation, and I like sharing my most intimate thoughts with you.

As I already told you during our tour of the Prado Museum on our very first outing alone, Mamá and I do not live like husband and wife and have not for a long time. When we came back from Madrid this time, she started sleeping in the guest bedroom, and we have never mentioned a word about it. We are both happier this way. She says I snore and keep her up. I do not need much sleep anyway, never have. I do not like to spend my time between the sheets, unless there is lovemaking, of course. I would much rather live among sheets of paper; my writing and you are my life right now.

I remember when you told me how good-looking my hands are, full of big veins and strength. I cannot even recall the last time Mamá gave me a compliment. On the contrary, she takes great pleasure in pointing out my shortcomings: I am bald, my nose is too big, I am only pleasant when other women are around (of course, unlike her, other women appreciate me). We spend entire days without speaking.

I am saving my true communication for you. I would be desperate without your letters to look forward to.

Tu,
Juan José

3 de octubre 1973

Queridísima Amparito,

I have been so concerned about you since you told me that Alberto is acting suspicious. Do you think he suspects that you and I were seeing each other last summer? If at any time you feel threatened, stop writing to me immediately. Perhaps you could send me a quick note to alert me, but I would not answer you until you were sure that the coast was clear of Moors (never was the Spanish saying so true: there are Moors with big ears).

Mamá is going to be away visiting Inmaculada and the granddaughters for a few days. She will take advantage that Inma is coming for the liver biopsy and go back with her. It will give me a few days of rest, which I terribly need. Every day there is some emergency, some errand or a doctor's visit, and my concentration is broken. Sometimes I feel like a lackey running around serving Her Highness. And the worst part is that I am not appreciated at all. She never says muchas gracias, and she sighs profusely when she has to cook or clean the dishes, as if she were being killed. It is just terrible.

I am glad you feel close to your daughter. Inma is supposed to take after me, but she is more like her mother than it appears. They both control their emotions. You know how I feel about that: if someone does not show emotion, it is because they do not care. I know that Inma is not happy with her soldier husband, even if he left the army or whatever he was in (once a soldier, always a soldier). Yet in every picture she sends (and she is always sending some), they all have these big smiles American style. Mamá says that I do not smile in pictures because my teeth are crooked (typical, ¿no?).

You, however, have a very pretty smile. Not phony. If someone wanted to guess why you look so happy, we would be in trouble.

I will not write any more until I hear from you.

Siempre tuyo,
Juan José

29 de octubre 1973

Mi querida Amparo,

You are so fetching when you are upset. I do not mean to say that you are not intelligent. Just that you do not have a formal education. If you had been with another kind of husband, instead of the bigheaded Alberto, you would have learned a lot. I could see how you took it all in when I was explaining the history of the Austrian Empire in El Escorial. Besides, I have told you before that I do not like know-it-all women. In fact, they make me ill. I guess I am a believer of the old Spanish saying: if a woman knows Latin, she will not catch a husband nor end up well.

However, you could read some contemporary novels, and I am sure you would enjoy them very much. Mamá had not read a complete book before she married me and has since become a great reader. Sometimes, just to humor her, I discuss a book with her. Why don't you read Five Hours with Mario by Miguel Delibes and tell me if you understand it and what you think about Carmen, does she remind you of anyone we know? (I could be Mario, ¿sí?).

Mamá is coming back in two days. I could have rested without her, but I have been having trouble in the department. For a long time, I tried not to get involved in its politics, since the capo di tutti, el profesor Walker, has been so good to me. He offered me a great job opportunity (just when I could not stand to live in Madrid another year) and negotiated my permanent visa as well. But there are certain things that one cannot leave unsaid. The Latin American professors want to bring in another specialist, but I put my foot down. We have enough of them. If they want another person, they could hire someone else from Spain, but no more linguists or Caribbean folk. They are taking over the academic world, and it makes for a less professional department. Why, pretty soon we will be dancing the samba over here!

Be careful, be careful, be careful. I worry that you are going to be found out.

Siempre tuyo,
Juan José

11 de noviembre 1973

Mi querida Amparo,

No sooner was Mamá back than she became ill and had to be admitted to the hospital. We had some awful, anguished days. There was no one there who knew Spanish, and I had to run back and forth trying to speak to the doctors. Talking to them on the phone is practically impossible. They hardly ever call back, and I cannot understand them anyway. To make matters worse, Rosa (you remember her—she and her husband Fernando were with us in Madrid) is upset with us and did not go to visit her at the hospital. Now Mamá blames me for having lost a friend, one of the few she had here.

You tell me if I am not right. Fernando voted with the rest of the department to bring in a Cuban professor, knowing full well that it was not what I wanted. This, after I brought him over here and Mamá and I treated them like family when they arrived. So much for friendship. I was so furious after the department meeting that I have stopped speaking to him, not even to say hi. I'm sure he has forbidden Rosa to speak to Mamá too. This is something else for Mamá to throw in my face, instead of agreeing with me as she should do if she were a good wife.

No, I do not think it would be possible for us to go to Spain for Christmas. Not the way Mamá feels and with the bad weather at that time of year. I can see that you miss me so much already, as do I, but we have to be reasonable for the time being. It looks as if we will be going to Atlanta to be with the granddaughters and the consuegros. I do not really care for those two, but I have to put up and shut up (¡muy difícil!). Imagine if Constance stopped coming by too. Mamá would kill me.

I now stop by the supermarket on my way home from the university. Can you imagine your husband doing the family shopping? It is not so uncommon here, and I do save some time running back and forth. I do not think I ever told you that I was the furriel during the Spanish Civil War. Sí, I was in charge of finding whatever food I could: snails by the streams, fruits and vegetables in the abandoned land; I even hunted rabbits. Good training, I guess, for my present life as the housekeeper. Every day I have more and more responsibilities. Then, when company comes, Mamá acts like she has been doing all the work (she does the cooking, but that's about all).

And who is taking care of you? I do wish we could be closer all year instead of waiting until the summer. Take good care of yourself, until I can see you again,

Juan José

9 de diciembre 1973

Mi querida Amparo,

¡Ay, ay, ay! You are so reckless! What in the world made you think that calling Junior to help you with the passport was a good idea? Luckily, he called when Mamá was out at the hairdresser with Constance and I was able to settle him down. No, no, no, I do not think you should come to "take care" of your sister-in-law. First of all, you have never traveled abroad and you do not know English. Do you think that coming to the

United States is like going to Paris or London? It is more like going from Valencia to Moscow. Now I am concerned that Junior is going to be more suspicious than he already is. Sí, sí, sí, I know he likes you too, but he will not the moment he finds out what your intentions really are.

I have come running to the office to write this letter. I was afraid that Mamá was going to come in and find me. Por favor, do not do any more crazy acts. The semester ends in early May, and I will make sure that we leave for Spain immediately. So after Christmas, it is only four months and we will be together.

In case you do not receive another letter from me before the holidays (the mail is more unreliable than ever this time of year), I wish you now the best, the most, and the least: the best food, the most love from me, and the least from your husband. I will make sure that Mamá sends a card to your family, the same as the years before, although she does not seem to be in the mood for anything.

Siempre, siempre, siempre, tuyo,
Juan José

3 de enero 1974

Mi querida Amparo,

¡Feliz Año Nuevo! We arrived yesterday from the family trip. I thought I would go crazy. First, the drive over with the consuegros—they are so smug. Talking about people as if they were taking roll call, no one escapes their radar. Thank goodness Paul Senior is a fine driver because we ran into an ice storm, and it was very dangerous. We almost had to stay over on the way, but it cleared during lunch. Second, Inma and the girls, all smiles and chatter. Mamá and I love our granddaughters, but they are too much for us now. It is nonstop noise and games. Then the soldier, I absolutely do not care for him. He is always judging people and looking at me with his piercing blue eyes. The worst part is that Mamá and I had to share the bedroom, and we really got very little sleep. I know she is not well, but she saves all her complaints for me, and she can be frankly hostile when no one is listening.

I stayed alone when they all went out shopping or took the girls to Christmas shows, and read sitting in the yard under the pine trees. I thought a lot about you. What kind of a life could we ever have together? And do not, por favor, think that I am asking you to leave your family and run over here. I am afraid you are capable of doing that and more. I am a lonely man and I have been for years now. Sometimes I feel that I have already said good-bye to my wife. The woman I married has already died; she has become someone else. Por favor, do not judge me. I am capable of pure, unadulterated love, but I need affection back. Love can die when it is not reciprocated. Believe me, I know it well.

I did not mean to turn so morose. I leave you now.

Tu,
Juan José

20 de febrero 1974

Querida Amparo,

Forgive me for not writing sooner. I am suffering the worst days of my life. Mamás condition has been deteriorating fast. She is acting very strange, aggressive almost, and she is definitely angry at me. The doctor explained to us that her liver is failing and it is not filtering properly. Her blood is poisoned by the time it reaches her brain. I fear to go out with her anywhere other than to her doctor's appointments. Now they are talking about admitting her to the hospital and giving her a complete transfusion. Inma is coming over in a few days. She is hoping to take her mother to Atlanta, if the doctor allows it. There is an important hospital at Emory University where they perform liver transplants, and they could evaluate Mamá. At this point, I am desperate and I welcome any help.

I have not been able to work on the book I promised to my publisher by May. I cannot concentrate. My classes are suffering as well. I have never enjoyed planning them too much, but now I find myself in front of the classroom, and I have no idea what we did the day before or what we are going to do now. I fear for my job.

Of course I love your letters, but you have to understand what I am going through. Mamá's illness is always on my mind. Not even when I am asleep can I rest completely. I wake up in the middle of the night dreaming that she is not sick and she is staring at me with her disdainful look, judging me.

I will write in a better mood next time, I promise you,

Juan José

* * *

17 de abril 1974

Señor Alberto Sastre García
Calle del Apostol Santiago, 23
Valencia, España

Estimado Alberto,

Last week, Junior called me from Madrid to inform me that you and Marlena found out that Amparo and I have been writing to each other for a few months. I take the liberty to write to you now to plead for some understanding.

First, I want to assure you that there never was any physical contact between your wife and me. I have the most sincere admiration for Amparo, and I would never take advantage of her nor insult you, my brother-in-law. Our correspondence was born of an innocent family relationship. Amparo has been helping me take care of your beloved sister with her wisdom and concern. You have to understand my situation here; I am in a foreign country, with a very ill wife and without family or friends to give me a hand.

I can imagine your anger at the thought that your wife has betrayed you, but she has not, would not; and I myself would not have allowed it, either. We were just two lonely souls without a physical body trying to support each other in a difficult time. Por favor, por favor, por favor, believe and understand this.

If I could, I would only ask you, again por favor, to write to me letting me know that you have forgiven our transgression. I hope you accept this letter as proof that I will never write nor speak to your wife in the future—that is, unless you allow us to in the context of our family relationship.

Yours truly,
Juan José Abello de la Torre

III

A mere two months after Inma's mother's death, Inma's father called announcing that he'd like to come to Atlanta to visit during spring break. Laura and Andrea were quite excited about the prospect; among other things, they were eager to show him their new dog. Inma and Paul had finally given in and bought them their first pet, a spunky Scottish terrier named Sir William McDuff ("Willie" for short). Laura, in particular, was sad whenever *Abuelita* was mentioned. She understood the finality of death and treasured anything her grandmother had made for her. Even if some of the sweaters no longer fit, she was determined to save them for her sister. And if she couldn't be with *Abuelita* anymore, at least she could spend some time with her Spanish grandfather.

Inma wasn't really looking forward to her father's visit. She had read and reread her father's letters to Aunt Amparo. Sometimes she even laughed out loud, provoking Paul's anger, who didn't see anything funny in them. But she mostly wavered between being furious at him for his unfaithfulness and feeling sorry for him for his naiveté. Inma had cried in frustration and sadness, but she didn't want to dwell on the letters anymore. To a certain degree, she understood what had taken place, even if she didn't condone it. But she was sure that a confrontation would be unavoidable when he came.

Since their trip to Madrid for *Abuelita's* funeral, Inma hadn't seen her father. They had spoken on the phone just a few times and only in a perfunctory way. She had submerged herself in her schoolwork and planned to graduate in May. She would prefer having her dad come then, since she regretted that her mother would not get to see her reach that goal. Inma could still hear her words: "Even to sew on a button, would have been better to have a degree first." She had already been admitted for a master's program at Emory University, and she knew that a change was taking place inside her. There was no going back now; Inma would become one of those women with higher education that her father despised.

Paul was beside himself. Each time they discussed the upcoming visit, they'd end up arguing.

"Your father is a perfect asshole. Why would you want to see him again?"

"If I can forgive him, why can't you? What has he done to you?"

"He has never liked me. He could do anything to anybody and not care. He's completely selfish." Paul wasn't about to give up.

"Selfish or not, he's my father. He's the only relative I have this side of the Atlantic, and I'm not going to break with him now. We don't choose our parents according to our tastes, right?"

"Okay, I can see it coming. Now we are moving to 'what is wrong with my parents'—one of your favorite subjects." He was a master at escalating an argument.

Inma excelled at hiding her conflicts from her daughters, or so she thought. By the time she drove to the airport to pick her father up, she was tied up in knots, a nervous wreck at the wheel, anticipating some possible scenarios. After all, she remembered her father mentioned something about having another story to tell her. What could he be up to now? She didn't put it past him, or her aunt for that matter, to have made plans to move Aunt Amparo to the States. Instead, Inma hoped that this visit would normalize her family into whatever configuration it was going to take without her mother. She rationalized that it's better to have one parent, or even half a parent, than none at all.

It was always surprising to see her father at a distance. He had a way of moving that made him seem much younger than his sixty years. If his head was covered with a beret, as it was this day at the airport, he looked twenty years younger. It surprised Inma that she was glad to see him. Her heart leaped inside her, and she smiled in his embrace.

"You look great, *Papá*. I guess being a widower agrees with you," she said.

"You are too thin, Inmaculada. Don't tell me that now you are on a diet like all the American women." There was no hiding that he came from the old Spanish school that equated thinness with bad health. "Why didn't the girls come?"

"Laura is at school, and Andrea is waiting at home with a babysitter. I drove straight from the university."

"Oh yes! I forget that you are fast becoming an educated woman," he said, trying to hide his sarcasm.

"*Papá*, don't start with your stupid comments." But he couldn't help himself.

Just at that instant, Inma noticed his sneaky squirrel look. "*¿Qué pasa?* What's going on? Do you have something to tell me?"

"It depends if you want to hear it or not. The last time I offered, you didn't want to know." Inma just looked at him expectantly. "I'm not coming alone, someone you know is meeting us at baggage claim. I hope you don't mind."

Now she knew that she was in for a surprise. He really was capable of anything. He stood erect on the escalator, carrying his briefcase, looking back with his crooked smile to read Inma's expression. She followed him silently, without smiling, through the long corridors full of people moving rapidly, going somewhere. It seemed that she traveled only for family visits, on emergencies, or on their many moves for Paul's career. Inma imagined what it would be like to get away for a break to a warm beach, just on vacation. She felt almost nauseated from the smell of fast food permeating the air.

"What's wrong? You are so quiet," her father probed, smiling still.

Before Inma had a chance to answer him, her father was greeting a tall woman, nearly as tall as herself. She looked familiar, but Inma couldn't place her right away. It wasn't her aunt, that was for sure. And she wasn't one of his students either, since she seemed to be middle-aged, though very attractive.

"You remember June Walker, don't you?" Inma's father was saying. "From the university in Indiana."

"Yes, how are you?" And then Inma realized who she was. June had even organized a bridal shower for her and her campus friends in what seemed ages ago. She was married to the chair of her father's department. He wouldn't dare, Inma fumed. The wife of his sponsor, his mentor in the States, the person who had been instrumental in her family's move to the United States! Inma stood with her while her father looked for his suitcase. June had a small carry-on with her.

"Your father assured me that it would be all right to meet him here. I'm coming from visiting Colleen in North Carolina. She's in college now." Inma was glancing at June's hands to see if she was wearing a ring. What she saw instead, adorning her wrist, was the gold bracelet her father had bought in Madrid when her mother died.

"Oh yes, I remember babysitting Colleen when she was a little girl," Inma said politely.

The three of them walked to the parking lot, looking for Inma's car, making inconsequential conversation. Inma felt cold despite it being such a warm day in Atlanta. Her mind was racing back to the years she'd spent on the university campus—first as her parents' daughter, later as a coed, then nearby in order to be close to her mother the year Paul had been in Vietnam. She hadn't thought about those years in a long time. It was as if that part of her life belonged to someone else. Now here was her father bringing it all back again. Paul was right; her father was a perfect asshole. This time, Inma made up her mind. She knew exactly what to do.

She drove away from the airport toward the downtown area. "June, have you ever been here before?" she asked politely. "You'll like Atlanta. There's a lot to do, and the weather should be lovely, much warmer than Indiana." Inma's father seemed so pleased with his daughter's perfect manners.

Inma took a center-city exit and pulled her car into the drive of the Hyatt Hotel. Her father hadn't even noticed the change in route. In the rearview mirror, Inma could see her father and June sitting in the backseat cozily talking to each other, holding hands like teenagers. She stopped the car and got out, opened the trunk, and put their suitcases on the curb for the valet to retrieve them.

"June," Inma said calmly, opening the back door, "it isn't you. I hope you understand. It's just too soon. I have nothing but good memories of you, but it's only been two months since my mother died, and my daughters and I are still grieving for her." And then, turning her head toward her father, she added, "*Papá*, give me a call, and I'll bring the girls over to the hotel. Laura is dying to see you. *Adiós, Papá*."

And she drove away by herself this time, not looking back even once.

AMERICAN WOMAN

I

Oh, thank you, Sylvia. It means immaculate in Spanish—pure, like the Virgin. Although I'm not so pure anymore, and I'm glad.

I appreciate your seeing me so soon. I'm so distraught.

That's right. As I told you over the phone, I am afraid. I feel threatened by my husband. That's why I made the appointment to see you.

No, not in so many words, but he makes a point of checking the drawer in his bedside table every evening to make sure the gun is still there.

I suppose it's legal since it's his service revolver. I guess he didn't have to return it when he left the Marine Corps.

No, I don't think it's loaded, but I can't tell. I'm afraid to touch it. I'm pretty sure the bullets are still in his trunk, "Big Bertha," as he calls it. Paul brought them back from his tour of duty in Vietnam.

The trunk is in the garage. It's quite large, one of those made like a wardrobe with drawers, a fold-down desk, and all. It's been there since we moved to Philadelphia over three years ago.

Okay, let's see. We've been married for fifteen years.

Yes, we were married very young. I hadn't finished college, and he had just graduated from Officer Training School in the Marine Corps.

No. It's the first time I've seen a therapist, but I've threatened to do it for a long time. I've known that we've had problems for years.

We've moved around a lot. This was our eleventh move. We've lived all over the country, mostly the South and the Midwest, with a stay in California too. First in the service, and then with corporate life, which is just about the same story, but in civilian clothes.

No, not really. In fact, I think we're still married because we moved so much. In some unexpected ways, moving is good for a marriage. At least for ours.

No, I'm not kidding. We were always busy with all the listing, selling, buying, closing our homes, and then packing, unpacking, measuring, painting, decorating, ordering furniture; and this was even though we always bought "move in and enjoy" houses. It's not like we were into "handyman specials." There was simply no time to get to the real issues. It begins with getting the mail rerouted; sending the change-of-address notices; settling the girls in a new school; finding new doctors for them and for me, dentists, orthodontists who are willing to adjust out-of-town braces; locating a compatible hairdresser, a good cleaners; starting all the services: housecleaning, lawn-mowing, window-washing, termite inspections. By the time all these chores were done and the girls had joined a softball league, the Bluebirds, and a dance school, it was time to start all over again. The family joke was that I didn't have to clean an oven or a refrigerator for the first twelve years of marriage. How lucky could I be? We moved instead.

Yes, Paul did some things. But his joke was that in all those relocations, he had yet to meet a mover. He did all the financial arrangements, which I know are not easy. He usually took care of starting the utilities and the telephone. He always settled our bills too. And, of course, he had to get used to his new job.

Sorry if I didn't get to the point. I guess I get my storytelling ability from my dad. I was saying that all the moving around kept us out of trouble. I have friends who blame the transient nature of the military and the corporate world for their breakups. Not me. We probably would have split by now if we hadn't been so busy moving. Besides, we didn't have many acquaintances, and we had to rely on each other. By the time we got settled, family and out-of-town friends started visiting us to see how well we were doing. All their comments to me—"I don't see how you do it," "Your house always looks so beautiful," "You are such a natural"—filled in nicely for other disappointments.

You know you're in trouble when your oldest daughter asks you, "Where am I from, Mommy?" and your youngest wants to know, on her first day of kindergarten, "Are we Jewish?" Oops, you mean to tell me that we forgot to give our children an identity, that we haven't been to church yet?

Then my mother's death was a pivotal point for me. She always told me that I should have finished my education before I got married. She was right, of course.

But everything became more complicated when I decided to go back to school to finish my degree and, afterward, to continue on to graduate school.

Well, I had to do all these wifely duties plus find a PhD program, attend classes, take exams, do research, write papers, teach.

I am a teaching assistant at the University of Pennsylvania. We teach one class per semester in exchange for tuition remission and a small stipend. I'm writing my dissertation now. When I finish, I plan to look for a full-time teaching position.

Yes, of course Paul knows that. We often argue about money, although my degrees have not cost him a cent. But the real problem is not my upcoming financial independence, as you suggest. I think he'll welcome another salary.

Our real problem comes from our—I don't know what to call it—our sexual independence, our sexual experimentation.

That's right, let's leave that for next time.

Okay. I'll do as you suggest and take care of the immediate problem first. Thanks for your help.

Yes, I know I can call you anytime. I'm already glad I did.

No, it wasn't so intimidating. I'm just not as confident as I appear.

*　　*　　*

Yes. It worked out just as you predicted. I picked up the girls at school and drove to our friends' house in Delaware. I had left Paul a note, so I didn't call until Saturday morning. I made it very clear to him: either he put away the gun or we weren't coming back and I was calling the police. Now I have Big Bertha's key. I'm holding on to it for safekeeping.

I think he was furious, but he kept it to himself. He couldn't believe our friends knew about our problems. The two of us have tried very hard to keep up appearances as a happy family, and then I go and do something as drastic as this.

We met Pam and Bill on vacation in Mexico. Bill was a big help. He actually got on the phone with Paul and explained the situation for me, about how frightened I was. I'm sure he's also on Paul's shit list now.

I'll be glad to tell you about our sexual escapades. Paul and I weren't very experienced when we got married. My mother used to say that I married too young, but she wasn't talking about my sexual history, of course. I realize now that Paul was always more interested in sex than I was. He was the one suggesting new things, and I often felt inadequate.

Like being a bit rougher than I wanted during our lovemaking or using sexual toys. He brought this thing called *ben wa* from Hong Kong, for example. Do you know what it is?

It's this heavy round ball women insert in their vagina, and it vibrates. It seems that Asian women wear it for long periods of time, even all day. It's supposed to stimulate you and make you more receptive for intercourse.

I realize that it could be sexy, but it just made me feel self-conscious. I think that he, we, missed the sexual revolution. While other people our age and younger were busy enjoying free love, he was dropping bombs, fighting a war in Vietnam, killing children. Paul used to say that if they bombed the orphanages first, they wouldn't have to fight the men later. And I was raising children at home. Then he, we, tried to make up for it.

Yes, I went along with it. In part because there was an implicit threat that if I didn't, someone else would. The truth is that he was content only for a while, and then he wanted to try something else. I'm sure some other woman, sexier and more daring than me, would have made him happier.

He is the restless sort. My father, who's never cared for him, calls him *un culo de mal asiento*, something like an ass that doesn't fit in its seat. As soon as he left the marines, he let his hair grow long. Then it was a perm. Soon he was wearing a necklace, bell-bottoms, hippy shirts. I started to go braless to please him. He tried playing the banjo for a while. We both smoked marijuana. Actually, I liked it more than he did—I don't want you to think that I'm a Goody Two-Shoes.

No, we never bought it, not even once. It was everywhere. Many of our corporate friends were using it at parties. Our babysitter must have noticed when we arrived home stoned. Hopefully, not our children.

We also played strip poker at parties. You know how that goes, right?

Mostly I felt embarrassed afterward. I got the feeling that we were always stalking our friends, checking which couple would be game for our games. Particularly when we started switching.

Exactly how many times? I don't know—nine . . . or ten. It was with three different couples.

No, we didn't switch with them because Pam was expecting then. Besides, Paul really doesn't care for her anyway.

Well, it was a turn-on of sorts for a while, but it only lasted a short time. Soon we were back to our normal ennui. I don't mean to minimize it, but a lot of it was the times. The *Bob & Carol & Ted & Alice* syndrome. Did you see that film?

Of course it caused problems; it quickly turned into *Carnal Knowledge*. Have you seen that one? There was jealousy and all kinds of comparisons. He would make me relate a play-by-play account, but that was the last thing I wanted to hear from him. I would just as soon not know what was happening in his encounters.

I knew he had become infatuated with one of his secretaries, a young woman who was married. He had also rediscovered his favorite single cousin. In fact, he went to visit her a couple of times while he was on business trips in New England.

I guess I really didn't care anymore. His favorite titillation was a very trampy Italian waitress with red hair, but he could never take her to the office, as he could his wife, and introduce her to his boss, although his friends knew about her; and that's how I found out she existed. That is when he proposed that we have an old-fashioned, "normal" affair, whatever that means.

Yes, I was game to a point, but I felt paranoid, as did he. We didn't want the girls, people at work, or our families to ever find out. So he started making all these "rules of engagement."

Oh my god, they were endless! He was still giving military orders. It couldn't be anyone from work or a close friend. We could never bring him or her home. There had to be total disclosure, which I already told you I hated. Absolutely no falling in love—it was supposed to be purely sexual, period.

Didn't I tell you it is a miracle that we are still married?

Yes, I've thought about it. In my mind, I know we are going to end up divorced, but neither one of us wants to take the first step. It's like we are waiting for the other to make a very bad move so that we can assign blame.

Actually, he thinks that I'm in love with someone else.

No, I'm really not, but I do have a special friend. His name is Agustín del Río, a Spanish man. I can't wait to tell you about him

Try it. *Ah-goose-teen*. Agustín. It's not too difficult to pronounce.

*   *   *

I'm getting braver all the time.

Well, I have my own checking account. There isn't much money in it, but I have one. I've ordered my own credit card too.

No, it hasn't arrived yet. I've also opened a safe-deposit box, and I have the trunk key, my passport, the girls' passports, birth certificates, and other important papers put away.

I told you I was paranoid. I don't put it past him to threaten me with anything he could think of. I also saved the rule sheet there.

For the affair. I thought it could be useful if we ever make it to court.

In a nutshell? I guess after so many years of being forced to act independently, I'm becoming independent. I didn't want to. I just wanted a normal family, whatever that is. Did I tell you that a few months ago, we started going to church every Sunday while all this other stuff was going on?

He's even an usher and a lay reader. It freaks me out to see him up there on the podium reading the gospel lesson the morning after one of our sexual escapades. I swear this is some sort of thrill for him. That's kinky, don't you think?

Yes, I've told him. Now it's become one of his lines: "Tell Sylvia this" or "Are you going to tell your therapist that?" It's a form of braggadocio, I think.

Not so much. I guess I'm at the point where having a husband who earns the money isn't as important to me anymore. It just isn't one of my priorities. I'm planning to look for a good teaching job. Do you know there are over thirty colleges in the Delaware Valley area? I wonder if Paul remembers that when we relocated here, I swore up and down I'd never move again.

Well, since the girls spend at least a month with their grandparents in Maine, I've been going to Spain by myself during the last two summers to do research for my dissertation.

It's on a contemporary Spanish writer. I have interviewed him two times already. I've even given a paper on his work at an international congress in Berlin. In fact, that's where I met my friend, Agustín. Yes, Agustín, not "Gus."

He is not really my lover.

Yes, we are having an affair. Well, we started having an affair anyway, but our sex was lousy. Ironic, isn't it? Besides, he lives in Germany and I'm here.

He is Spanish; that's a big part of the attraction. But like me, he has immigrated to another country. We have a lot in common, and he likes me just the way I am. I don't have to do anything else or agree to any rules. I feel that he is my friend unconditionally. This is what I told Paul, and I wish I hadn't. He says I'm in love and that I've broken the rules.

I told him that I'm not playing any more games and that I'm entitled to have my own friends. From now on, I decide who they are and for how long.

Yes, it started that way. I came home at the end of my trip last summer, and Paul was waiting for me at JFK. I rattled on about the affair the entire ride home. I know it was a big turn-on for him; I think he's creepy.

What do you mean by latent homosexual tendencies?

Oh my goodness. Paul would go crazy if he heard that. He thinks he's Mr. *Macho Man*.

Okay, I'll continue. We both were on the same panel giving our papers, and right away I felt attracted to him. Actually, he looks a bit like Paul, which makes me creepy as well, I know. He just seemed familiar to me from the very first minute I heard him speak. We both try to keep our native tongues sharp to camouflage all the years we have been away from Spain.

No, no sexual pun intended.

The entire panel went out to lunch together. Agustín was our guide since he lives there. He loves Berlin as much as I love Philadelphia. We ate at a popular sidewalk café with a glass enclosure on Alexanderplatz. We sat next to each other and joked the entire time, entre nous. Have I ever told you that Paul never makes me laugh?

It's a cultural difference. We just don't find the same things funny. He likes bathroom humor—which, by the way, he's passing on to our daughters, and I just hate it. I find pleasure in word games and repartee.

Yes, in three languages. Where was I?

Okay, I'll see you next week, then.

*   *   *

Sorry I'm late. Andrea is home sick, and I had to wait for the sitter.

Are you kidding? He'd never take time off work. My degree seems like a hobby to him. He likes showing off in front of the people at work, though, about how I'm getting my PhD.

Yes, the affair. I think I mentioned that all the *congresistas* had lunch together. From the restaurant, we went straight to his flat near the university. We were in bed before sundown. Neither one of us drinks much, but we were high from our conversation and our mutual discovery.

He did perform this first time with a bit of hesitation that I thought was just nervousness. I was nervous too. I went back to the hotel in a taxi. We had made arrangements to meet the next morning at the congress; we'd decided to pretend that we ran into each other after a session. All very silly, I realize, but tantalizing nevertheless. Right after lunch, we went back to his place, and I could tell right away that he was more interested in talking than in sex, which was fine with me. I told you we are soul mates. Or are you going to tell me that he has some latent homosexual tendencies also?

Do you want to know what I think?

I'm pretty sure that he wasn't completely truthful with me. He's not as separated from his wife as he initially told me. His kids were with her in the home they have in the Pyrenees, north of Barcelona. But Agustín's place in Berlin felt like the kids live there as well. When I asked him about it, he told me that, of course, they have joint custody. Anyway, I think he felt guilty when he saw how earnest I was.

No, I don't mean in love. I mean happy to have an equal as a friend. To be able to mention an author, a book, a song, an old cartoon, or a Spanish movie and have him understand immediately what I meant. Do you know that I had never made love in Spanish until that summer?

Yes, I know. It wasn't great, but he would perform on and off. Very unpredictable, it's true. We saw each other every chance we got the rest of the week. I bet people did notice it.

I'm sure we weren't as discreet as we thought. I flew back to Madrid, and he was there in less than two days. We were both staying with family. It was ideal, almost like dating. We saw *Luisa Fernanda*, a zarzuela, a Spanish operetta, all very folkloric.

Two years ago, I wouldn't have been caught dead at one, but I loved it. I cried over the protagonist's moral dilemma and over the ridiculous happy ending. We walked in El Retiro Park, next to where I grew up. We ate in popular restaurants where I had never been, although they were all within walking distance of my house.

I didn't need to worry. My family wouldn't be caught dead in any of the places we went. Actually, we ran into a professor from the University of Pennsylvania at the Reina Sofía Museum, and I introduced Agustín to him as if not being with my husband were the most common thing in the world. I don't think I blushed. It's not like I was worried that my husband would find out. In my mind, I was still behaving according to the rules.

The problem is that I have stopped following the script. Agustín and I have been writing since the summer, and I've refused to share the letters with Paul.

Well, he knows enough Spanish to figure it out, but not enough to get it right. And he's imagined the worst. Besides, I have already gone over the allotted time for an affair.

I didn't tell you that rule? Six months max. Wait until you hear this. It gets better. Before Christmas, Paul wrote to Agustín, inviting him to join us for the holidays—as a "surprise" for me. That's right. Luckily, Agustín wrote immediately, telling me about it, and I confronted Paul with it.

I'm not sure. Once, he told me that he planned to hire a thug to beat him up when he arrived in New York.

Then he said he was "just joking." I can't tell anymore, but I don't put anything past him. I just don't trust him anymore. And it's mutual, of course.

Yes, we've continued writing. It's a matter of principle. I'm not going to have anyone dictate what I can and cannot do. It's that simple. As Paul says, I've become "unruly."

Now I have plans to go to Spain again this coming summer, but I'm afraid.

He claims that if I go, he'll expose me. He'll never allow the girls to live with me. He'll tell his parents, the works.

I can say that he started it all, but who is going to believe me? As Paul says, a hot-blooded Spaniard against a churchgoing American—whom do you think they are going to trust? If they only knew that neither one of us fulfills the stereotype.

I have to think about it. What do you suggest I do?

Of course, I have to decide myself and suffer the consequences. Sometimes I think that it was easier when I had a script to follow, when Paul told me exactly what to do and I did it.

Not really, but you know what I mean.

That's true. There will always be something he can hold over my head. It's not like we don't have anything to hide. It's a mess, but obviously, I'm not going to stay in the marriage just because I'm afraid of the consequences.

* * *

It's been an awful week. Willie, our Scottie, bit the little girl next door on the lip, and she had always dreamed of becoming a model. I feel just terrible.

The kids were upstairs; it was the one hot day we had, remember? They were dressing the dog in a tutu and he just snapped. He's always been hotheaded.

The insurance will cover everything this one time, but we have to get rid of the dog. The girls are devastated. Luckily, their grandparents are going to adopt him. They've always had dogs, and that way, the girls will be able to see Willie once in a while. They're coming by in two weeks to take the girls to Maine, and they'll pick up the dog then too.

Really. They have always been very good that way. I can still count on them in an emergency.

Sure thing. I made the reservations already. I have five weeks this year. I'll be in Madrid first, and then I plan to meet Agustín at his place in the Pyrenees. Not bad, huh?

I'm not going to tell Paul. He'll have my flight information and my brother's number in case of an emergency, but that's it. I'm sure he's been making plans of his own.

I told him that he has as much to hide as I do, and that he'd only hurt the kids that way. Do you really think that Paul could ever take care of the girls by himself?

It's like a roller coaster. One minute he's threatening me, and the next he says that we need to get back on track. I don't see how. I'll be looking for a job as soon as I defend my dissertation.

In October . . . I don't have the exact date yet.

Yes, I do. I think I've come a long way. Thank you, Sylvia, for helping me out.

I know it's been almost a year since "Gus," as you call him, and I have seen each other. But really, we are not in love. We are just good friends. He has been very supportive about my new assertiveness. He's given me the confidence I needed to break away from Paul. I doubt I'll be able to stay with him for more than a week. His "ex-wife" is arriving with the children.

What can I say? I'm the one who is still "officially" married. Sometimes I think Agustín is scared of me. He's even less free than I am.

He has all kinds of commitments during the summer: his kids, his supposedly ex-wife, his parents, while I probably won't see my father for more than an afternoon.

Yes, he is in Spain for the summer. But I really don't want to talk about him. He's married to a young student of his. Someone who was doing her master's under him . . . get it?

She's a sweet woman; I feel like she could be my daughter sooner than she could be my stepmother. It's very odd, but then I'm done trying to understand my father. There was a time when I truly cared about what he thought. No more. I have bigger fish to fry, don't you think?

It's scary, though. Sometimes I think that I'm more like my dad than I want to be. Did I tell you there is someone else I'd like to meet while I am in Europe?

That's right. Maybe I'll finally have a real affair. I'll make sure to call you as soon as I get back. Who knows what kind of trouble I am going to get into this time?

I hope so. Again, thanks so much for everything.

* * *

II

Summer 1981

Sábado, 11 de julio

Here I am, finally, on the plane. I'm going to keep a journal while I'm not seeing Sylvia. I'm having a hard time concentrating on the book I wanted to read. I keep thinking about our pseudo-reconciliation last night. We are both being so dishonest that I really don't know anymore when I'm being true to myself (as Sylvia says) or when I'm playing games. It's a matter of time, I know. As soon as I can make it on my own—financially speaking, that is—I'm going to push for a divorce. Of course, when I say that I want to separate, Paul says that he wants to work on our relationship; if he mentions it first, I start backtracking too. I think we are both afraid of being alone after so many years of companionship, however flawed it's been.

We went to the movies, ate out, and had sex (I can't really call it making love anymore). I couldn't concentrate then either. I just lay there and pretended that I was having an orgasm when I wasn't even close, as I have done so many times before. How's that for not being true to yourself? I bet

Paul wouldn't even believe it if I ever told him how unfulfilled I feel despite all our sexual shenanigans.

Things are simpler when the girls are not around. I was sad for a few days after they left, but I needed a break from them too. The truth is that if I stay home and write these next five weeks, it'd give a big push to my dissertation, but instead, I'm off to do what? Find myself? I have this feeling that I'm still doing things out of order. I should have traveled around before I was married and had children. There is this saying in Spanish: "A la vejez, viruelas" (To have chickenpox at an old age). That's good; I'm getting my old Spanish wisdom ready in preparation for this trip. It's as if my mother were still buzzing around me.

Just to confirm all my doubts, when we were ready to leave for the airport, right after lunch, Paul started a fight, asking me for the key to my safe-deposit box. I wouldn't give in, and he could sense it too, but he had to push until we were arguing again. It's easier saying good-bye this way, when we are angry at each other. Thanks, Paul. Then, just as we said good-bye, he asked me not to do anything that would damage our marriage even further, which made me feel terribly guilty, given my plans.

Sitting next to me is a young couple from Modesto, California, on their first trip to Europe. They are so sweet to each other; they've only been married two years. They make me nostalgic for a more innocent time, even though Paul and I were never like that, traveling together to Spain on vacation. They are watching this dumb movie, *The Idolmaker*. Maybe that's what I should have done since I haven't even been able to read my book.

Domingo, 12 de julio

The flight arrived in Madrid early, and there wasn't anyone waiting for me at the airport. It isn't the first time. I have to accept that my comings and goings just aren't as important to my relatives as they are to me. At least Puri, the maid, knew I was coming and was expecting me at my brother's place, so I was able to unpack and get some rest. Every time I come to Spain, I realize how privileged they are to have live-in help. Sometimes I think—only half jokingly—that I would trade a husband for a maid on a moment's notice.

I'm not good at being alone when I travel, so I called Lita as soon as I woke up from a nap. We have been friends since we were little girls. She's had this boyfriend, Maxi, for a long time, but they don't live together; nor does she plan for them to. He has two children from his first marriage "and a mother," Lita always says, with emphasis on the *mother* part. There is no way she's going to marry now and end up taking care of someone else's mother. Hers, like mine, passed away a few years ago.

We took a walk through El Retiro Park and ate at La Florida, close to Alcalá Street. It's always this way; we don't see each other for years, we don't keep in touch while I'm away, but whenever we get together again, it's as if we had seen each other just yesterday. I share with her a more normal version of my relationship with Agustín; that is, I add more sex with the boyfriend and less with the husband, as it well should be. Lita looks as trendy as ever, with platinum blonde hair and a nose job, which makes her even more attractive than she already was. We joke around that it's too bad she isn't a guy, we get along famously.

We walked by the Palacio de cristal on our way back. This is one of my favorite spots in the entire park. The building is almost transparent. The small lake in front of it is full of swans gliding from side to side. The reflection of the tall waterspout on the building makes it look as if the roof had opened up and was breathing water. The branches of the weeping willows caress the lake and, at times, hide the silent swans. There is an exhibit of Henry Moore's sculptures, some inside the palace and some in the gardens, flowing quietly from space to space, blending glass, bronze, and water.

By the time my brother and his wife arrived tonight from their summer home in the mountains, I was so jet-lagged that I couldn't stay up and talk to them for long. I haven't yet seen my niece Pilucha because she's spending the month with her grandparents, just like Laura and Andrea are. I can't keep my eyes open. I'm turning off the light now.

Lunes, 13 de julio

This morning, I met my father at his favorite bookstore, Espasa-Calpe. I swear he likes it so much because everyone recognizes him and fusses over him. They showed him how his books are prominently displayed. I like Crisol better, a much younger place where they wouldn't know an old fogy like my dad.

I got even, and then some, over lunch. His wife joined us at another Old World spot, La Trainera, an overpriced seafood restaurant. The waiter began by calling me *señorita* and Marielle *señora,* despite the fact that she is several years younger than me (that'll teach her to play Eliza Doolittle's role). My father proceeded to correct the waiter, explaining proudly that the young lady is his wife and I, though older, am his daughter. Luckily, in good Spanish tradition, the waiter knows his place and is not used to making small talk with the clientele. He continued calling us according to what he could see, never mind the relationship. My brother and I had a good laugh when I told him the story. Then I was sad because I realized that Junior and our father haven't seen each other practically since my mother died.

In the afternoon, I met with Jesús F. Santos again. I was able to ask him concrete questions this time since I'm so familiar with his work. I can tell that he's pleased with my progress. Turns out that someone else, in Connecticut, is also writing about him. The pressure is on for me to get my dissertation done. Then a very awkward moment. As I went to kiss him good-bye, cheek to cheek, he stuck his tongue in my mouth instead. I was too shocked to say anything and ran down the stairs, ready to throw up. The *langostinos* from lunch mixed in my throat with the taste of liquor and tobacco reeking out of Jesús's mouth.

What's with these Spanish men? Immediately, I started thinking that somehow I had asked for this lewd behavior since I told him that I was seeing someone, and that my husband and I are talking about separating. I've decided to keep this unpleasant incident to myself for now.

Days are so long over here, particularly in the summer when it's light until almost ten in the evening. That and the fact that they don't go to bed until one or two in the morning makes me feel like I'm here a week for each passing day. This evening, there was still time to go to the movies with my sister-in-law to see *Bodas de sangre* by Carlos Saura. I just loved every minute of it. I realize that now I am more sensitive to Spanish dance—even flamenco—since I've met Agustín. He was supposed to call today, but I didn't hear from him. I've asked Puri three times already, and I'm afraid that she is suspecting something. I'm trying to go to sleep, but I'm upset about Jesús and wondering about Agustín. In the summer, since Pilucha is away, they use this room to store the Oriental carpets, and there is an awful odor of naphthalene, which makes me sick. I miss my home already.

Miércoles, 15 de julio

Agustín called yesterday, first thing in the morning, and we made arrangements to get together next Monday. I'll fly to Barcelona, and we'll drive together to his place in the Pyrenees. He sounded good with his deep voice and thick Castilian accent. But I didn't feel an electric current going through me, as I had hoped. It was about as exciting as making plans with Lita, which I also made for today. In part it's because I feel apprehensive and I don't want to get too excited for fear I'll be disappointed.

I also had a conversation with Jesús F. Santos. He's inviting my dad, his wife, and me for dinner on Saturday. I don't feel at all like seeing him again, but I can't say no without an explanation. I've concluded that he was drunk and didn't even know what he was doing, but from now on, I'm acting American and shaking his hand; no more kisses anywhere.

I've been reading more and taking good notes. A soon as I get back to Philadelphia, I want to start writing again without delay. I'm nurturing an idea for a presentation.

What if I illustrated *Paraíso encerrado* by F. Santos with slides? It all takes place in El Retiro Park, which according to its title is an "Enclosed Paradise." I already have a visual image in my head of each story. I wish Jesús hadn't been so disgusting. It makes it hard to separate the man from the writer.

As usual when I'm in Spain, I'm not sleeping well. It starts with jet lag and it runs into anxiety, this time with very good reason. What impact is my relationship with Agustín going to have on my marriage? There's no going back. Last year it was part of the crazy agreement with Paul, but this year I'm on my own, and I'll have to live with the consequences, as Sylvia has pointed out. I'm so busy during the days here that I don't seem upset or worried, but as soon as I try to sleep, it's like a film projected onto my closed eyelids. Another one of my mother's sayings comes to mind: "La procesión va por dentro" (the parade is going on inside). It doesn't work at all when I translate it into English.

Viernes, 17 de julio

I've been doing lots of errands: I bought my ticket for Barcelona at Iberia in the Plaza de Neptuno; opened a bank account in Banco Central, past the Plaza de Cibeles, around the corner on Alcalá Street; and renewed my Biblioteca Nacional card, just up the boulevard on Castellana. It helps that every place I go, someone recognizes my last name. They know either my father or my brother or both. It's the opposite in the States, where no one can even pronounce *Abello*. On the other hand, several people have made comments about my accent sounding American. I can't win; I'm a foreigner in some way or other, wherever I am.

Yesterday afternoon, I went to the cemetery with my brother to visit our mother. It was such a hot day that the place was completely deserted. Even the flower stands were closed. In the summer, the entire city seems to shut down after lunch. The cats must have been sleeping as well, although I could smell the strong, acrid stink of their urine. The flowers too smelled stronger than I remembered. We walked in silence through the labyrinth that has become familiar now. The gray marble plaque over my mother's niche still looks brand-new despite the more than six years that have passed. What would she say if she could see me now? I can't imagine she'd like the twists and turns of my life at all. Yet I'd have to tell her that, as unsettled as my life is, I'm happier now than before I started to stand on my own two feet. I don't know what's going to happen, but I prefer this uncertainty to the past tediousness.

My brother and I don't really connect. He is not in touch with our father, and since I am, he mistrusts me. My dad feels that way around me too. I hate being caught in between, yet I refuse to stop seeing either one. I'm entitled to have both a brother and a father, but I don't truly have either one. This breakdown of our family would be the most upsetting for my mother to witness. Where did we go wrong? Was it the uprooting effect of immigration, or do all families go through such unsettling times?

I decided to call Paul and I reached him at home, but with the time difference, it turned out that I woke him up. He sounded sad, almost depressed, and I felt terrible. He hasn't been feeling well. He's been to the doctor, who has done some tests and has diagnosed him with hypoglycemia, something to do with his low sugar level. The girls are having a great old time in Maine. He'll be joining them and picking them up just before I get back. He didn't ask me a single question, and I didn't volunteer any information either. We were both true to form.

Sábado, 18 de julio

Today is the anniversary of Franco's uprising against the Republic. It used to be a big holiday when I was growing up, but now, conspicuously, it's ignored by the democratic government. However, there are groups of young neo-Nazis demonstrating all over the city. They are wearing the dark-blue shirts of the Falange party, raising their right arms while they chant the Fascist hymn: "Cara al sol con la camisa nueva . . ." (Facing the sun with a new shirt on . . .). I left the house with my camera, thinking I'd take some pictures, but it was too intimidating. I felt uncomfortable, so I went back to my brother's place in Niño Jesús rather upset by the whole thing. Suddenly I felt old. What do these punks know about Franco? They didn't have to live under his censorship as my generation did.

My dad called midmorning to say that the biggest demonstrations were taking place where Franco is buried, at El Valle de los Caídos (the Valley of the Fallen) near El Escorial, where my father lives. The road to Madrid had been closed, and he was afraid to take the train into the city, so our dinner with F. Santos is postponed until tomorrow. I'm not surprised he feels that way. He fought in the Spanish Civil War and was shot at by people wearing the exact same color shirts. It has to be very painful. When I told my brother and his wife, they laughed at him and called him *rojo*, the term associated with the Republicans.

It amazes me how quickly plans are made and unmade in Spain. Lita and I decided to go to see *Evita*, which is playing in Atocha. I saw it in Philadelphia and adored it; but, I don't know why, hearing it in Spanish is so much more moving. Patxy Axión plays the role of Che Guevara. Now he gives me the chills, so I'm not dead yet. My friend and I ended up having a late dinner in La Gran Vía and laughing like we used to do as young girls when we cut school to catch a film. Is it possible that we saw *Davy Crockett* together then, as she says?

Domingo, 19 de julio

I spent the morning getting ready for the trip tomorrow. Washing and drying my long hair takes forever with the travel hair dryer. Packing just the right clothes is another silly dilemma. I don't want to carry too much, yet it's colder in the Pyrenees and I want to look my best. I'm quite nervous. Thank goodness my brother and Clara have left for the mountains. The truth is that I should stay in a hotel when I come to Madrid, especially for this sort of trip. I can't expect to carry on like a liberated woman in the midst of my family, sleeping in my niece's room, which used to be my own room as a child. I must be nuts. Finally, Puri left too, and I had the place to myself for a couple of hours.

The dinner at F. Santos's home was a pain in the butt, literally. I was sitting tensely on a hard chair and couldn't wait to be miles (well, kilometers) away from Madrid. My father dominated the conversation and appropriated the books that Jesús was offering us too. I must admit my father is witty, especially next to that insipid wife of his. I found myself laughing even when I didn't want to. He told that joke I've heard him tell many times before about the dirty old man who applies for a new driver's license, and when the cute policewoman filling out the form asks him, "Sex?" he says, "If you insist."

I'm thinking about F. Santos also as a dirty old man, but he hardly paid any attention to me. I was sure he wouldn't risk a repeat performance with my father around. They made plans to go together to his hometown in León later in the summer, and I made a point of saying that I was otherwise engaged. Maybe I am acting like a bit of a tease. I've got to stop that.

There was a rare summer storm while we were finishing dinner. I heard the rain and the wind whipping the tall windows. I had never seen Madrid at night from a high-rise like this. The fact is that I like this city in any light, at any distance.

I have no idea where Puri is; maybe she's staying out all night. This is not a democratic country for nothing. I can't get to sleep. What if I don't like Agustín anymore? And if I do like him, it's even more of a problem. What am I going to do, wait another year until I can see him again?

Lunes, 20 de julio

It used to be that I did my best thinking in airports and I could read while flying, completely isolated in the midst of crowds. No more. I believe that tells me something: I have a guilty conscience, for example, and I cannot put my situation out of my mind. I'm like one of those swans in El Retiro Park. I look cool and collected on the outside, but I'm pedaling fast as hell underneath.

Since it's Monday and the middle of summer, there is all kind of traffic going to Barajas. According to my new profile as a liberated woman, I didn't ask my brother to take me to the airport and he didn't offer, either. Despite all the tension I feel, everything went smoothly with the short flight to Barcelona. I arrived on time, and Agustín was waiting for me with a broad smile showing that sexy space between his front teeth. He looked good; he's tan already, and he exudes health, humor, and confidence. His beard has more gray in it than I remember from last year, and when I told him, he said that's because he's been worrying about me. Cute!

Right away, we started our bantering. He said that I have an American look about me, although I was wearing a new outfit I had just bought in Madrid's El Corte Inglés. Maybe he said it because I'm taller than he is. I even sound American, according to him. He likes to call me *Conce* since my namesake is the Immaculate Conception. So I started calling him *Gus*, as Sylvia does, the gringo version of his name. In fact, he also looks foreign, German really, with his too casual attire and rather pushy attitude. Not to dwell on stereotypes, but I'm certain both of us have assimilated the ways of our host countries, whether we want to or not.

We spent the rest of the morning looking for a hotel. We had to leave our bags in the lobby of the Regina since the room was not ready yet. A simple detail like this could have made a big difference. Let me explain. I'm sure we both were very happy to see each other again, but by the time we had eaten and walked around Las Ramblas in the hottest hours of the day and he'd had a couple of beers too many, our mood had changed. It didn't help matters that when we went up to our room, neither the toilet nor the shower was working properly, and we had to wait until they took their sweet time sending someone to fix them.

To be frank, it was also my fault. As soon as we got in the car from the airport, I started to give him the entire lowdown about my situation with Paul: the gun, the threats—a more detailed version than the one I wrote in my letters to him. I think I scared him. He listened to all of it sympathetically, but he must have thought that I was ready to leave everything behind and move to Old Europe, which couldn't be farther from the truth. I may like to play around in Spain, but I've been thinking that I couldn't live here anymore.

Barcelona feels much more like a small town than Madrid. Either that or Agustín shouldn't have chosen the most popular restaurant in the Barceloneta district, where his brother-in-law was also having dinner. That was the last straw to break our romantic mood: *la vie en famille*. Turns out that Agustín's kids are vacationing with his sister; otherwise, we'd have run into them too. There just wasn't a spark when we finally went back to the room for the night. We are like distant cousins; we can flirt and tantalize each other, but we'd need a papal dispensation to make it as a couple. We didn't even try making love, which made me angry in some way and relieved in another. Being a man, he slept rather soundly, but I was even more awake than in my brother's house.

Martes, 21 de julio

At breakfast this morning, we talked about our feelings and decided to spend the week together as we planned, but just as good friends, which we now agree we are. I didn't tell him then, but I couldn't have taken the steps I took if it hadn't been for him. So we are not lovers, but maybe it's better this way, difficult as it is not to take it personally.

The drive up the Costa Brava is just breathtaking. It was a sunny, clear, warm day. The road is full of sharp curves, which offer deep views of rocky cliffs with small pine trees hanging on for dear life, and then a bright blue patch of azure water at the bottom. Each little town we passed had a marina with too many boats, too small a beach full of bathers, and too many cafés to choose from. We ate lunch in Portbou, which, true to its name, is just beautiful. We felt exhilarated and sad at the same time. I wish we could also click in bed, but then it would be too unreal, too perfect. Could there really be a happy ending?

We drove on into the Pyrenees as far as the French border in Cerbère. We stopped at every turn so I could take pictures, which, Agustín says, is also very American. I have the feeling that these pictures will have to sustain me for a long time, the same with my travel journal. I assured him that if I hadn't left my tape recorder in Madrid, I would also tape our conversations. I feel like one of the trees on the side of the road, holding on to life while it's precious. From what he tells me about his children, he's probably a great father. He seems to know a lot about adolescence. And here we are (or at least, I feel like I am), acting like two irresponsible people. He gets angry when I tell him that and doesn't agree with me at all. Aha! So he does preserve his quick Spanish temper. He wishes our children could meet and we could all spend time together as good old friends. Sure, I'll see what I can arrange for next summer. He must be nuts!

We talked a lot about literature too. He loves Francisco Umbral, and I don't. He thinks F. Santos is repetitious, and I agree. I told him about his "French kiss." Turns out that it's not called that in Spanish at all; it's "morrear, darse un morreo," something like to put the snouts together, which sounds so pedestrian to me. Perhaps I would know the word for it if I had a chance to practice on a live subject, I told him.

Then we bought some food in Figueres to take to his place in the evening. It seemed that everyone was doing the exact same thing. The main square, the little shops, the rustic sidewalks were all mobbed. Young children, dressed alike as if each group belonged to a clan, were screaming, chasing one another. Spanish kids are the loudest I've ever heard, very cute but bratty. I don't see how their parents can stand it. I miss my girls, so well behaved and sweet, even if they don't want to wear matching outfits.

I can't believe this happened to me again: in the midst of the big commotion in the center of town, we had to run into another of my professors at Emory and his wife. How is this possible? I guess that's better than if we saw someone from the University of Pennsylvania. Here I think that I'm doing something so original and fun, but it's just part of the academic schedule. Well, the part about summering in Spain, that is. Now that I really don't have anything to hide, I'm a nervous wreck. Agustín thinks that I'm charming when

I get flustered. He accused me of liking my old teacher. I got even by telling him that I wouldn't get involved with another Spaniard at any cost.

I like Agustín's place. It's rustic—he had warned me—but it's also comfortable and welcoming. It was dark by the time we arrived and I couldn't see the lake, but I felt the humidity rising from the water and heard the wind rustling tiny waves in the night. I'm staying in Eva´s room, Agustín's daughter; it's tiny, but comfy. I guess I can't escape from this little-girl role just yet.

Miércoles, 22 de julio

Despite all the complaining about my insomnia, I woke up when the sun was quite high. The birds were making a racket outside; otherwise, I'd have slept even longer. I could smell bread baking. Now that's something new—a man who can make bread. So we won't have to go back into town today and run into old beaus, Agustín said. The reflecting light from the lake is so bright that, much to Agustín's mirth, I had to wear my sunglasses inside the house. From where I was sitting, there was a cool breeze coming from across the mountains—la tramontana, it's called. Agustín wanted to go parasailing on the lake. I passed. I said that I'd rather take pictures and read in the sun. I'm finishing up *Paraíso encerrado* by F. Santos. In contrast, this is an open paradise.

It was just about the most perfect day I've seen in a long time. I could smell the pines warming up in the heat of the morning, but as the sun hid behind the tall trees, I needed to put on a light sweater. It seems that the breeze picked up a bit very fast, and soon Agustín had disappeared around a bend. Occasionally, I heard voices in the distance, but I didn't see another person until Agustín came back for lunch. We ate a simple feast of *pan con tomata,* his bread with olive oil, tomatoes, and *serrano* ham. He washed it down with wine, but I had fresh lemonade because I didn't want to feel sleepy in the afternoon after waking up so late. I wanted to wring the last possible drop from this day.

I'm almost sure that Agustín is still married. There are certain feminine details in this place: the terra-cotta pots with geraniums all around the house, the orderly kitchen compared to the rest of the rooms. He laughed at me and said I'm too rigid. Whoever said that men couldn't plant flowers? Besides, he already told me that he shares this place with his ex because both spend time here with their kids, and yes, sometimes they are here at the same time as well. I let it go. I'm married too, and my situation is not conventional either. I've promised myself not to ruin this precious time with any more confessions and questionnaires, even though I want to confide in him about François and the possibility that I may make arrangements to see him before I return to the States.

We've been sitting by the fire reading since a late dinner of lamb chops and salad. I told him that I don't want to cook and mess up his ex's kitchen. At least I know how to make this man laugh, even if I don't turn him on. What's wrong with him? Sorry, no questions.

Viernes, 24 de julio

Yesterday, we took a drive to see the Teatro-Museo Dalí in Figueres. It was the most fun! I've always been interested in Dalí, with all his surreal inventions and iconoclastic turns.

Now I really like it—not just his works, but the way they are displayed in such original installations in this museum. Seeing his work where he was born and lived makes it more meaningful. The town looks completely different without many people during the day. Isn't it weird that everyone comes out at the same time in the evening? Agustín says that no one would be caught dead in the heat of the day except tourists. He has a way of poking fun at me. He has to be such a local that he's wearing *alpargatas,* the peasant-type shoes made out of grass. I've told him he looks like a country bumpkin. We ate outside at a small place in the plaza in a shady spot. It is really all quite charming.

I took advantage of the moment and called the girls in Maine. Even though it was early there, I knew they'd already be up. It was low tide, and they were digging clams with their grandfather for a clambake in the evening. Their voices sounded distant and sweet, and I could hear Willie barking in the background. As Laura said, there was an echo between us. Constance asked about my family, and I felt guilty. Not because I am with Agustín, but because I'm not spending any time with relatives. I haven't even seen my niece. How can I say that I miss my family in Spain so much? Leave it to my mother-in-law to ask just the right questions.

Coming back into Agustín's place later was such déjà vu, as if we had lived here together for a long time. We bought flowers for the table, bread and fish for dinner. He had a small accident cutting some wood for the fire. I've noticed that he's often bleeding somewhere. That's what it must be like having a son, not that I ever want to find out, that's for sure.

I decide to tell him about my tentative plans to visit François. At first he was shocked that I had even considered getting together with someone else this summer. But then he claimed to understand that I'd want to go see Paris, where I've never been. If we are only friends, as he keeps reminding me, why should he care? Deep in my mind, I knew I wouldn't find what I was looking for with Agustín. And what is that, sex? I don't even know. Not sex, but sexual attraction. It's clear, though, that I'm not going to spend the time I have left visiting family.

Agustín says that he's going to drive me back to Madrid, and he'll show me some other beautiful parts of the mountains and the city where he is from on the way.

Sábado, 25 de julio

We were not in a hurry to leave this morning. We were both sad. We have a nice friendship and that is a good thing, but we could have had something more. I feel waves of anger coming over me, but I don't want to show Agustín, and as is characteristic of me, I keep it all in.

Once we were on the road, we were fine again. The scenery is so beautiful that it's impossible to stay in a bad mood. There are small green valleys with clear streams running through them. It seems that every inch or centimeter of land is cultivated. From the distance, it looks like an abstract chessboard. The mountains are so tall, they reach into the clouds and disappear. Small herds of sheep and goats are grazing here and there. The houses are made of gray stone with slate roofs, dark shutters, and lovely flowers in the window boxes. Occasionally, a solitary goat is tied up by a back door somewhere.

We stopped to have a late lunch in Ainsa, a typical town with ancient walls and hilly narrow streets. The corn was already gathered, tied up in big bunches, ready for the winter months. We bought some local *tetilla* cheese, shaped like small tits. I noticed that the women have strong legs with short calves, from years of climbing in the countryside. I'm so aware the trip is coming to an end that I want to take pictures nonstop. I don't know when I'll ever be back this way again. I'm afraid I've ruined a roll of film in my haste to catch some shepherds coming into town with their animals.

We arrived in Huesca, in the foothills of the Pyrenees, almost at sunset. Agustín had made reservations at the hotel Pedro I de Aragón, and this time, we have a lovely room with twin beds. We were both tired and lay down to rest a bit. He asked me if I wanted a massage. I know better, but I said, "*Claro que sí.*" I couldn't tell if he was making a pass at me or not, and I didn't want to assume anything and be disappointed again. He has a soothing and gentle touch. He said I was tense. I warned him that he was making me horny, so he stopped. I guess we both knew what that means.

Huesca is a very charming city, all lit up at night. The old part where we are staying is full of churches and a beautiful Gothic cathedral, which was still open. We went inside to admire the *retablo* and the remains of the old Romanesque cloister. I could see that Agustín enjoyed showing off his city. I imagine him as a teacher, and I'm sure his students admire him. He's only a few years older than I, but he's farther ahead in his career. He didn't stop his education for ten years as I did. We ended up having dinner at the hotel restaurant. We want to get up early and drive straight through to Madrid tomorrow.

Lunes, 27 de julio

The drive to Madrid on Sunday was like a long good-bye. We talked a lot and tried to make sense of our time together. I suppose we need distance to understand it better. Agustín loves driving in Spain, much more than in Germany, he says. The roads are not nearly as good, but it's always more interesting. I never drive in Spain since I'm petrified of the crazy drivers and I can't drive a stick shift. I would much rather take trains, planes, or even buses, as we used to do when I was a little girl and we didn't have a car. Agustín plans to stay in Germany as long as his teaching career lasts and then to retire in Spain, possibly in his home in Figueres, which he would then fix up. He wouldn't want to live in Madrid or any other big city. I have no clue where I'll end up. Soon I'll be looking for a job, and I'd like to stay put for a while, hopefully in the Philadelphia area.

When we arrived at my brother's place, we used the excuse that there was no place to leave the car and said good-bye standing on the street. It was both awkward and sweet at the same time, like a first date when one has the feeling there won't be a second one.

Junior and his wife are staying in the mountains for a few days, and Puri has taken off on vacation too, so when I arrived, I found myself living alone for the first time on this trip. For a second, I thought of running out and calling Agustín back. Maybe we could have shared this place for a few more days. But it was only a fleeting fancy.

There is very little food around, and everything would have been closed at this time on a Sunday. Luckily, there were some eggs in the refrigerator, so I made myself an omelet. I read, I write in my journal. Lita has left town on vacation. I tried calling Paul, but he didn't pick up. It isn't so odd that he'd be out on a Sunday afternoon. What surprises me is how very little I've thought of him these past few days. I had one of the best night's sleep I've had in a long time. This morning, I called François at his office since he had said I could. The secretary picked up, and just as I started using my French, she changed to English. He called back almost immediately and seemed very excited that I would be willing to come to Paris. He had been in touch with our friend Selena and he knew I was in Europe, so he wasn't totally surprised. I only met him that one time at my neighbor's house in Philadelphia, but I've heard her talk about him many times. He's a bachelor, at least ten years younger than we are. I wonder if she's had an affair with him because she's always commenting on what a bon vivant he is. He was planning to leave on vacation, but he seemed more than happy to change his plans and lend me his studio apartment. He'll use his family's flat while he shows me Paris, at least for a few days, but I can stay as long as I like. He sounds like a perfect gentleman to me.

I went running over to the Iberia offices before they closed, this time for a ticket to Paris. I'll be there five nights. I'll need time back here in Madrid to buy more books and work on the *Paraíso encerrado* project.

This is so unlike me, yet it isn't. I've always wanted to travel. What's unlike me is not feeling sad or brooding about Agustín or barely worrying about Paul. I'm ready for a new escapade.

Jueves, 30 de julio

I must be nuts, traveling again on just about the busiest day of the summer. Half of Europe is starting their vacation this weekend, and here I am on my way to Paris.

I don't know why, but for the first time in my adult life, I take off my wedding band. I guess I don't want to be seen as a married woman when I'm acting this way. I practically don't know François, but I know I'm playing with fire. Selena told me that he studied in the States, where she met him; that he has lived in Brazil for a few years; and that he just recently moved to his own place in the City of Lights.

The last few days in Madrid have been quiet and restful. I did speak with Paul on Tuesday, and he seems to be feeling better. He doesn't need any medication to control his "condition." It's a matter of watching his diet. He is getting ready to drive to Maine for a few days and pick up the girls. He didn't ask me a single question, and again, I didn't volunteer any information. I feel completely removed from his orbit. I can't imagine that we won't talk seriously about getting a divorce when I get back. Right now that's what I want, and I feel good about it because there isn't anyone waiting to catch me. It isn't that I want to leave to be with someone else; it's because of the way we feel these days. We can't live together anymore. Plain and simple. A big difference.

François was waiting for me at the gate. Despite the fact that he was wearing a suit, he looked much younger than I expected. He's very tall and thin, as I remembered. He has an expressive face, not handsome but original, with big features and an interesting dimple on his chin. We were a little stiff with each other, but then again, I have noticed that everything is a tad more formal here in Paris. It's quite a bit cooler, and people dress less casually than in Madrid. I noticed it even in the airport. I was glad I wore a skirt instead of my usual travel attire of jeans.

François drives a Mini Cooper, the tiniest car I've ever seen. And here I thought that the Seat 600 my family had in Spain during Franco's time took the prize. I don't know what we'd have done if I'd had a bigger suitcase instead of my carry-on. There was awful traffic all the way from Orly into the city, and it was misty and much darker than in Madrid at the same hour. We are farther north, that's why. We speak mostly in English. If I say a word in French, I have to repeat it three times before he understands it.

His place is on the ground floor of a gorgeous old building in L'Opéra Quartier, the center of town. There is a little patio with a gate to the street, with just enough room to fit the Mini in. He was telling me that his studio is almost finished as we were walking in, and I was speechless. Appropriately, it looks like the set for a French movie. It isn't that it's so fancy, but it's very classy. It has high ceilings and a marble fireplace with a tall gold mirror sitting on the mantle. The pièce de résistance is a contemporary, bright cobalt blue leather sofa. The same blue is echoed in a few art pieces (and later, I find out, in the bathroom towels and other linens). The kitchen is tiny, all done up in the same blue and white. Everything is just so. I feel a small letdown when I ask him who his interior decorator is and he says his mother. She's been deciding it all for him. Now I'm really glad I don't have sons. A daybed rests against one wall, half-hidden by a folding screen. When I first saw it out of the corner of my eye, I could tell that it was very narrow, covered with lots of pillows. "Don't worry,"

François said. "I won't be staying here. My parents' place is just around the corner."

Viernes, 31 de julio

I reread yesterday's entry, and I think that I should have been an interior decorator. I'm more taken by the studio than by the man. I'm waiting for François. He went to his office this morning for a short time, and then he's coming by to start our tour. I went out early to take a walk in the neighborhood. He said I couldn't get lost since he lives between two large boulevards, Haussmann and de la Madeleine. I did enjoy strolling through the small streets full of shops, most of them not open yet, and seeing people walking their dogs. That's something remarkable. There are a lot of dogs in Paris and thus lots of poop around. One must walk looking at the ground. I reached the beautiful Place de la Madeleine with its huge church. A lively flower market was opening up, and I bought blue hydrangeas for François's place. Something his mother had not thought about yet, at least not this week.

Last night we went for dinner to a fancy place on Rue Vendôme. We had a nice-enough meal. This time he asked a lot of questions about my life and family situation. I could tell he had heard a sneak preview from Selena. He caught me by surprise, and I blushed when he told me how beautiful I am. I can't remember the last time anyone told me that. He has impeccable manners. He's very sure of himself. I reminded him that I must be ten years older than he. He couldn't care less. We spent a long time looking for orange juice and some croissants for my breakfast. He hasn't used his kitchen yet, and—get this—his mother left on summer vacation before she had a chance to get some groceries for him. How could she?

I don't know what they call it in France, but before he left for the night, we French-kissed with gusto outside on the little patio. I wonder what would have happened if he had come in with me. I read for quite a while before I fell asleep.

Domingo, 2 de agosto

I must be a tramp. Since Friday evening, François and I have been making love in the small daybed several times, once on the leather sofa (*Mon Dieu*, if his mother only knew) and another time inside the tub (thank goodness he lives on the ground floor because the water spilled all over the place). On second thought, maybe his mother would be proud of her baby getting it on with *une professeur*, as he introduced me proudly to a neighbor.

I guess all the sightseeing was foreplay. We spent most of the day Friday in the de rigueur places: L'Opéra, le Palais-Royal, les Champ-Elysées, la Tour Eiffel. François wanted to take advantage of the clear day and leave the museums for when it rained, which is not so unusual in Paris this time of year. We had dinner in a cozy restaurant in the Place Dauphine. It's very easy to flirt running around in Paris. Besides, the kiss from the night before had opened all kinds of possibilities. When I offer him a taste of my soup, he says not to worry, he'll taste it later. Sure enough, it was dark when we finally headed back to his studio and we stopped to look at the Seine from the Pont Neuf. What is a sweet woman like me to do? Or am I sexy now? He's like an owl or a vampire who comes alive at night.

He's different from the other men I've known. The fact that he's younger has a definite appeal. His body is harder, he's thinner, I can feel his bony back. He is so eager, almost voracious. His lovemaking is completely unpredictable, and I don't mean that in the Agustín sort of way. His specialty is French love (whatever it's called here or anywhere else), and then there are the different places where we have already tried it. It certainly is not like making love to Paul, who is reliable but so predictable. Despite all our games, after more than fifteen years, it's become routine. I couldn't reach an orgasm with François the first time, and I wasn't about to pretend anything. Good move on my part. He took it upon himself to try even harder in a couple of hours. Very nice indeed.

Yesterday morning, we were at it again before we left on our tour. Okay, so he's not a vampire. When I woke up, he was sound asleep on the leather sofa. He had thrown a sheet over it, but he was naked. Despite his thin frame, his legs are muscular. He can be funny too. As I was tiptoeing around the room, he grabbed me from behind and there I was, caught in his arms again. Not only that, but he's also a fast learner. Now this routine I could get used to.

Sure enough, it was misting outside. I loved the drive to Fountainbleu, the two of us chatting like two characters in an Eric Roehmer film, despite some crazy French drivers who don't want to be second to their Spanish neighbors in anything. The gardens are so beautiful and soothing, all wrapped up in this wet fog. The inside of the palace I could do without. Now I know where the Spaniards get their taste. I can understand that La Granja, on the way to Segovia, is like a miniature Fountainbleu with fewer mirrors. On our way back to Paris, we stopped at Orly airport and changed my ticket so I can stay for three more days (and nights).

Last night we tried a Spanish restaurant, El Picador. A big mistake. The French may beat us at palaces, but we are better at paellas. At least it gave me a chance to get even, teasing François about his Spanish. So much for his sense of humor. After he's been correcting me nonstop, his feathers got ruffled when I talked to the Spanish waiter "too long." Wasn't this guy such a playboy? We went by Moulin Rouge and took a walk in Montmartre, which put us in a romantic mood again, although that area of Paris is not so beautiful, at least at night.

When I woke up this morning, he had gone out and left me a billet-doux saying that he'd be right back. I stayed in bed writing, and he brought me breakfast in bed. Do I need to say more? He's trying to give Paul a bad name. Turns out that Selena had told him all kinds of tales about him. Now my feathers were ruffled. I told him that Selena's husband is not what you'd call a great catch either. We are off to do more sightseeing again, and tomorrow I'll be on my own.

Martes, 4 de agosto

I guess my life is not like a French movie after all. Twenty-four hours after changing the ticket, I got my period. How's that for timing? I'm more upset than François. I had to wash the sheet by hand because he doesn't have laundry facilities. He takes his wash to his mother's!

I've decided that my favorite area of Paris is Le Marais, where I spent most of yesterday by myself. François got upset with me when I told him—he can be such a snob—but I guess it reminds me of my neighborhood in Madrid, with all its gardens, specialty shops, and small bistros. La Place des Vosges is as intimate a square as I've ever seen. I sat in a corner restaurant and had a leisurely meal while I read. Then I walked to the Hôtel Carnavalet. I was thinking that the girls would enjoy seeing this place. Laura is interested in city models, and this museum is almost like a dollhouse but in grown-up size. I'm pretty sure that François doesn't care for children very much. He changes the subject when I bring mine up. His sister has three, and he has commented how bratty they are. I bet he becomes jealous when his mother pays attention to the grandchildren. It's just a feeling I get. I did some shopping for the girls: some miniatures for their dollhouses and some hair accessories, which are just beautiful here.

Today I spent the day at Le Louvre, but it's just too much to take in all at once. I get the same overwhelming feeling at El Prado. My favorite museum is Le Jeu de Paume, where the French Impressionists are. It gives the Barnes in Philadelphia a run for its money. Paris is one of those cities that the more one gets to know it, the more there is left to do. And this has nothing to do with my tour guide. On the contrary, I've enjoyed my days alone in the city just as much, if not more; and besides, I get to practice my French—language, that is.

Jueves, 6 de agosto

I'm not sure what's going on. François is acting strange. At first I thought maybe he was put out by my period after all, but it isn't that. He says that I am a very sexy lady. Our lovemaking now is not as much fun for me because I'm self-conscious, that much I know. He did ask me to give him a hand job, but complained when I wasn't up to speed, literally. The fact is that I am exhausted. All this touring has caught up with me. Yesterday, in particular, I didn't feel well after running from one side of the city to another to see Beaubourg and Les Halles in the morning and then Cluny, Luxemburg Palace, and La Sorbonne in the afternoon. We stayed in last night and ordered Chinese food (yes, in Paris). It was so cold outside that I asked him if we could have a fire. Turns out that the fireplace is fake. He says he's very upset that I'm leaving tomorrow.

Today I went to his office, met some of his staff, and went out to lunch with him. He has a fancy setup in an old building that has been refurbished. He's one of a team of investors and market analysts. It's all Greek to me since I don't even have a job yet. It's a bit too soon to think about investing. I could tell that he wanted to show me off. Actually, he asked me to wear a skirt, which I was planning to do anyway (these men!). We did talk, for the first time, about my dissertation and my plans for employment. He's familiar with the American university system because he got an MBA at Cornell.

We are going out to dinner tonight, and I know he's planning something special. I'm going to take a nap.

Viernes, 7 de agosto

Okay, I think that François is falling in love with me! I can't believe this, the one who was supposed to be such a cool cat. The one time I don't get emotionally involved, to use Paul's language. It makes me feel so guilty, but I don't think I've led him on at all. We went to a very traditional, almost formal, Indian restaurant. First, he wanted to know if we could meet again next week in southern France so he could introduce me to his family. Then he gave me a gift. I was speechless. I opened the little box and it was a gold bracelet. I'm sure it cost a fortune. It's made out of real leaves (from Singapore, I think he said) that have been dipped in gold. I've never seen anything like it. It's not that I don't like it, which is what he thought. It's that I don't know what it means. I almost feel dirty, as if I'm being paid. He says he wants to make plans to visit me in the States. I reminded him that I'm still a married woman, but suddenly he didn't seem to know a thing about the American way of life. Yes, sure, I'll introduce him to my family. That should go over big!

And what about me? What do I feel for François? For me it has been something completely new. I have no regrets. I'm glad I came to Paris. Now I've had a real sexy affair—uncensored, spontaneous, and not sponsored by anyone. But this time is very different. First of all, I don't plan to tell a soul. Well, other than my therapist. Not Lita, not my sister-in-law—who is very curious about my comings and goings—and certainly not Paul, if he even cares anymore. I don't sense any of the emotional connection with François that I have with Agustín. I'm not sure that we'll even end up being friends. I felt bad for him last night. For the first time, he seemed so young and innocent, no matter how skilled his lovemaking is. He's frustrated since he's used to getting what he wants, but I'm not for sale.

I promised to call him from Madrid. In the airport, I thought for a minute that he would start crying. For the first time, he kissed me openly, without a cover of darkness. I was almost mortified, or was he making me sad?

Domingo, 9 de agosto

I called the girls on Friday as soon as I was back in Madrid. Talking about feeling sad! They both asked me when I was getting home. I thought they could never get tired of Maine and their grandparents, but I was wrong. It hasn't helped that their dad is with them, no surprise there. Paul didn't even get on the phone. Now I'm so anxious to leave and get my life in order. This trip is coming to an end, this much I know. I can feel the usual nostalgia before leaving once again. Yet I want to go home to be with my daughters, however topsy-turvy my relationship with Paul is now.

This afternoon I'm sitting under the pine trees in my family's mountain home while they are all finally taking a nap. My, they are a noisy bunch! I thought they'd never settle down. I can see the mountains in the distance and smell burning wood coming from the neighboring houses where they are still grilling their lunch. Yesterday, from the train, I could see the peaks of Guadarrama, still snow covered in the month of August.

Just seeing my niece was worth the trip. She's such a cute little girl, with a very round face covered with freckles and a little dimple in each cheek when she smiles. Being around her makes me miss my daughters even more. I'm trying to figure out if there is a family resemblance, but I don't see it. Maybe in the coloring, that contrast of very light skin and the dark hair, but not in the features, which are more angular in my kids. Pilucha looks almost Asian. This is her maternal grandparents' summer place. They seem so traditional, yet they are not. He's an expert at the grill, using different types of wood according to the menu. I noticed that today's lamb chops had a definite rosemary flavor. He's also a doting grandfather who often picks Pilucha up from kindergarten. The grandmother is still beautiful and has a commanding presence about her. She is nothing like my mother was, but seeing her interact with her granddaughter makes me sad, as if my mother had died recently, when it's already been more than six years.

Despite all the family tales we've been sharing over lunch, my father's name hasn't even come up. He's with his young wife just a few train stops down the mountains, but he's not part of this family's get-together. I'm certain it all would be so different if my mother were alive. I can't complain though because I won't stop to see my father on my way back either. I'll call him before I leave.

Martes, 11 de agosto

Yesterday, my last day in Madrid, I took advantage of the morning sun to shoot the slides for my *Paraíso encerrado* project in El Retiro Park. I'm very excited about this. In some ways, it's like a bridge between the young girl who grew up here, playing in this very park, and the woman I have become, doing a research project for my career.

I came in through the Niño Jesús entrance, up the shaded walk, covered by the chestnut trees, with benches that are full of lovers at night. The old guardhouse has been removed, but I found two remaining ones at the other end of the park by Atocha. The gardeners were watering the bushes, making colorful sparkles shine off their hoses. The wet dirt had the smell of a summer storm, rich and cool. I went past La rosaleda, the rose garden, where I used to play as a child, which looked somewhat dry but still fragrant with buds. Taking pictures of the statue of the fallen angel is easy now since traffic has been restricted. The statues of the fish spouting water out of their open mouths seem a lot smaller than I remember. So early in the morning, there aren't children playing yet; in the summer months, they usually come out to play in the cool of the evening. Just a few tourists were walking around the lake, probably waiting for the boat rides to start. King Alfonso XII on his marble horse still looks imposing, high over the granite steps. I've always liked the formal gardens, with their classical statues standing parallel (in the French fashion I now know) all the way to the entrance on the Calle de Alcalá.

I went by the Velázquez Palace, closed for repairs, which is going to become an exhibition venue. I only peeked at the Crystal Palace because I'd already taken pictures of it earlier this trip. It was as clear and bright as I've ever seen it, sparkling under the brilliant sun. The old zoo gates are still up, with the lion heads on top of the Moorish columns. This is one of the most unusual spots in the entire park—it's almost surreal, with some of the old empty huts remaining—since the animals have been moved to larger quarters in La Casa de Campo, a newer part of the city. I swear I could still smell the potent odor of the bears as if they had never left. Only the aviary is populated—not by exotic birds now, but by the urban kind: sparrows, swallows, pigeons. Some ducks have taken over the pond in the polar bear sheds. Next to the old zoo, there is an area I'm not familiar with. I think it was closed to the public before. Now it's a conference center, appropriate for weddings, with elaborate gardens, pergolas, and topiaries in whimsical animal shapes.

When I came out of the park, the noise of the traffic and the sight of the new high-rise, Torre de Valencia, hit me as if

I were waking up from a dream. Spain and my neighborhood have changed so much in the last several years. Sometimes I don't recognize them. When my family moved to the States almost twenty years ago, I certainly didn't know that I was leaving this enclosed paradise behind.

III

Oh my god! I sure do, I don't know where to start. First of all, the girls are home, they're fine. There never was a single word about them staying any longer or anywhere else. If anything, as far as they're concerned, I could have come back much earlier. They were as happy to see me as I was to see them.

Yes, Gus. We're still friends, but we definitely are not lovers. Neither are Paul and me. We haven't made love since I got home. Not even mentioned it.

No, we are sleeping in the same bed. Thank goodness it's a king-size and we don't have to get close. I guess we still are not ready to let people know. Especially the girls. To tell you the truth, we're not talking a lot these days.

The three of them came to pick me up in New York. That set the tone, quite a difference from last year. The girls were so chatty all the way home. Mostly we talked about their time in Maine and about my family in Spain.

That's right. It became obvious very soon that we are not blabbing about what we did in our separate sexual summer camps. Paul looks a lot thinner, almost sick, but he says that he's under a doctor's care and is feeling well. He's been on a diet because now he thinks he has hypoglycemia. Something new to complain about, I guess.

We've been taking care of a few things around the house, and the yard needed some attention too. I've been buying back-to-school clothes for the girls and getting ready for the start of the school year myself.

No, I don't have to teach this semester. I have these next couple of months to finish my dissertation and defend it. I'll be starting a job search as well.

It went well for the most part. The author I'm working on turned out to be a lush, but I got my interview finished. I have all his works now, and I've even started on a new idea for a future research project.

No, I didn't write a word. Well, aside from my travel journal, that is. I did that faithfully to keep me centered. I loved doing it. In some ways, it was like speaking with you.

Yes, I was very busy. Remember I told you I might go to see someone else?

Okay, I'll start with Gus, as you still call him. Just as I thought, we spent a week together, mostly at his place, but we did some sightseeing too. I thought we got along well, and he was supportive of what I'm going through. He's a great guy; he cooks, he gardens. He's like the boyfriend I never had when I was growing up.

Because just when I was old enough to start going out, we moved to this country. I'm an expert at skipping parts of my life and having to go back to fill them in. Next thing I knew, I was a college coed talking about getting married.

My mother used to say the same thing. Yes, of course I got married too young, but let me tell you that a lot of young women my age were getting married too. That's the way it was then. Their weddings took place right after college graduation. I married the wrong man or he married the wrong woman, probably both. That's the real problem.

No, I'm not looking for a husband, not even for a man; but let me tell you, I must look like a good catch. I haven't told you yet. This other guy I met keeps calling me from France. I have the feeling this could get ugly.

He's not happy with me because I'm not free to take his calls.

Paul is going to find out, and he'll figure a way to use it against me.

No, I met him here, in Philadelphia, last spring. He's my neighbor's friend, and he invited me casually to visit him in Paris. I wonder if he even thought I was going to take him up on it.

Yes, I did. I finally had my own affair *comme il faut*—sex and all.

No, other than my neighbor, I haven't told anyone. He's been in touch with her, and she had already figured it all out anyway. I think he's trying to enlist her help.

The truth? I was just having a good time. I felt flattered that someone younger, and supposedly more worldly, was so smitten with me. But I never said that I loved him, or even liked him, and he knows well that I'm still married. Now he's upset because I won't make any commitment to see him again. I don't even want to talk to him on the phone. He's a spoiled man, used to having his own way, and I'm not interested in him.

Yes, I like him as a friend. No, no, he's not really a friend. I liked having this affair, okay? But that's all. As far as I'm concerned, it's over.

Of course I understand there are consequences to be paid, although sometimes I feel that I've already paid for this dearly. Paul must have been carrying on himself, or maybe not, and that is why he's so sour.

I have been living under my husband's threats for a long time. He's been manipulating me, or trying to, for years. He was orchestrating all this sexual conduct.

Some were consensual, but not all. You know that. I felt pushed into it by him.

Fine, I'll be thinking about what responsibility I have for the demise of this marriage.

*   *   *

It's been awful. There's this tension building up. It's like we're both waiting to see who breaks down first. I feel that I can't breathe. I would have been better off teaching this semester.

I'm trying to write during the day while he's at work, but it's very hard to concentrate. He shows up unannounced, as if I were going to carry on at home. Perhaps he thinks that I'm still receiving letters. I get an upset stomach the minute I hear his Audi in the driveway.

Yes, we've been arguing, but only during these impromptu visits or when both girls are away from home, which is rare. When they are around, it's more like the cold war.

Yes, I've asked him how long he thinks we can go on this way.

I've asked him that too. He doesn't want to. He says it's bullshit. I've suggested that we get a new counselor so he won't feel that you are biased.

No, lately you seem to be on his side. I'm almost defending myself.

He's waiting me out. I know how he thinks. When I get my degree and find a job, he won't have to give me money. Other than child support, that is.

I guess I am. Yes, I'm talking divorce. It's not so surprising, is it? It's a hell of a lot more honest than the way we're living now.

It doesn't help that François called twice last week, in the middle of dinner.

That's right. That's his name. I'm very angry at him. I finally called him from my neighbor's house and asked him not to call again. I told him that I don't want to see him, that I need to put my life in order before I can entertain another relationship.

He was furious. He said that I didn't seem so worried about my married life or what Paul thought when I was with him, that I gave him the impression I was free. I've given a bracelet he gave me to Selena so she can return it to him next time she visits. That seemed to shut him up. Isn't that unbelievable?

No, I haven't heard from him again, but it's only been four days.

Yes? So you think I can tell Paul just as clearly that we need to talk? I'll try it. I know that I'm used to giving mixed messages or that I can be passive-aggressive, as you call it. Paul is aggressive-aggressive, I guess.

I don't want to piss people off, but I end up doing it anyway. You're right, I may as well be up front with it. Be completely honest with him.

No, I'm not going to tell him about the affair. I thought you meant the truth about how I feel about him now. He hasn't told me about his summer either. I have no idea what he's been up to, nor do I really care anymore.

I wonder, sure, but he hasn't been out of town or arrived home later than usual. I know he's worried about his job and the possibility of a transfer.

There's talk again about moving to Toledo, Ohio, but even he doesn't want to go there. The school year has just begun. The way things are between us now, he's not going to get me to consider it.

Yes, I know. Moving can be good for a marriage, to a point. The way our marriage has become, not even eleven more moves could save it.

Okay. I'm going to make an effort to get it on the table. I promise.

*   *   *

You'll be proud of me. I got a babysitter, we went out to eat, and literally, we put it all on the table. He wants a divorce as much as I do, maybe more. Now I do think there is somebody else.

No, it doesn't matter, really. I suspect someone at work. Anyway, he's writing down all the rules.

You know he's a control freak. It's his way to gain the upper hand. We've already agreed that we'll wait until after the holidays. First, there is my dissertation defense.

I didn't tell you? It's the first week of November, and I'm getting psyched for it.

Then comes Andrea's birthday. We don't want the girls to associate our breakup with any important dates.

I feel good about it. I'm relieved. I didn't think it would be this easy.

I know, I mean to get to this point. We also agreed on total discretion. He knows you're behind it, but we're not telling family or friends. The last thing we want is for the girls to hear it from someone else first.

That's about it for now. He's going to come up with a financial agreement.

I won't, don't worry. I won't sign a thing without an attorney. Is there someone you recommend?

Sure, I'll ask at school.

I did go to the doctor. He gave me some lithium. It's like Valium, I think. It settles my stomach down before meals. Sleeping has been difficult too, but I've always had trouble with insomnia.

I've also been sending my résumé out. Mostly to local universities, although I wish I could move once in my life for my own job. But I don't want to uproot the girls one more time, especially now. They both love their schools. At least I'll try it locally first. Guess where there is an opening?

In Toledo, Ohio, of all places.

No, I won't be applying there. It's not even a temptation to think I could move one more time, continue being married to Paul, pretending we are the all-American family.

The interviews are held at the MLA, the Modern Languages Association. This year it's in New York City, the week after Christmas.

We haven't made plans yet. We're going to a family get-together in New England right before the holidays. His parents are celebrating their fortieth wedding anniversary.

They love the girls, but I feel that they won't miss me. In some strange way, I'll miss them because I have no family to speak of in this country.

My dad remarried and we are not close. Everything changed when my mother died. She kept our family together.

Yes, I do. I have girlfriends at work. Of course we're all going to be looking for jobs at about the same time. Many are going to move away. Sometimes I think that the American way of life is very difficult. Most of my relatives in Spain live in the same towns, literally in the same homes, all their adult lives. My brother is in the house where we grew up as kids. It's a completely different mind-set.

I've actually been thinking about it recently, since this past summer anyway. I used to think that I'd go back eventually, but not now. My life is here, imperfect as it is. Just by coincidence, I was noticing that soon Laura will be exactly the age I was when my family moved to the States. My dad really thought he was doing something great for his family. No questions asked. He hasn't understood yet what happened between him and my brother. Where did he go wrong? Why did his only son go back to Spain alone? He has no clue about how uprooted we felt and how difficult it was for my mother too. He felt oppressed in Spain, but the rest of us didn't. We just had a normal life like everyone else we knew.

Yes, I do think I can be fulfilled here. Sometimes I joke that I'm happy only over the Atlantic, flying one way or the other, anticipating the part of my life I've been missing. It's like I'm never complete anywhere. But now my daughters are American, and I've become an American through them, in translation, so to speak.

I know it sounds bad in psychological terms, but it isn't that I'm living through them. It's that I didn't experience the same childhood they did. Didn't I tell you that I'm an expert at doing things backward?

That's right, I'll be a full-fledged doctor next time I see you. Wish me luck.

*   *   *

Thanks for seeing me on such short notice. Paul is a jerk. I've never been so upset in my entire life. Just when I felt that things were starting to work out.

The good news first: the defense went well. It was really a formality, just as everyone said. The worst part was getting the darn thing written and typed on time, according to the Modern Languages Association specifications.

Yes, we did, a celebration of sorts. Most of the other PhD candidates were there. Later we went out to eat, just the four of us. For a few hours, on the surface, it was as if we were a happy family again, but I was conscious of the subtext the entire time.

There is more. I have a job for next semester at Bryn Mawr College. Not too bad, huh?

Thank you very much. I don't know yet. They might have a permanent position in the fall. It depends on funding.

Well, out of the clear blue sky, just when everything seemed to be going smoothly, Paul shows up midday the day before yesterday and throws this big manila envelope at me. "Remember these?" he says with a smirk on his face.

It's a bunch of old photographs he took of me through the years.

No, they are not pornographic, but they are suggestive.

Yes, I'm naked in a lot of them, or is it "nude"? Is there a difference? They are compromising, I guess. I agreed to pose, or he would have looked for another model. I was supposed to feel thankful that he found me so alluring, but I always felt awkward doing it.

I called him an asshole, one of his favorite words. I've tried everything since then: pleading, crying, cajoling . . . nothing!

First, he said it wouldn't look good in a women's college if he exposed me. What irony! Then he suggested we get back together and try again to work things out. The latest is that he'll show the pictures to his attorney, and I won't have a chance in hell to get custody of my daughters.

Reconciliation? No, not at all. I'm through. This is hardly a basis for reconciliation. There's always going to be something else he'll try to hold over my head. It's blackmail, plain and simple!

For one thing, I've started sleeping in my study.

I told them that my allergies are acting up, that I don't want to wake Daddy up with my coughing. At least Laura suspects, I'm sure of it.

We are arguing constantly and not always sotto voce. I've called him a pimp, and you can imagine what his retort to that was. It's just awful. And here we are two weeks before Christmas.

No, thank goodness, they are not coming since we just saw them for their anniversary celebration.

It went fine. I felt like a hypocrite, though. I was trying to think about when we started faking a happiness that wasn't real, or does every family live in such a charade? There we were, telling little family anecdotes while hiding a separation agreement.

I guess I am. If having an overwhelming feeling of sadness is to be depressed, then I am. Am I supposed to be happy now?

Yes, of course there is anger. Actually, the meaner he's now, the easier it's to go through with our plans to separate. Except I don't even know if our schedule still holds or what.

And just how am I going to take control?

All right, I'll try that. I'll tell him that if he doesn't move out, I will. The thought has already crossed my mind. There is a guesthouse on the Bryn Mawr campus. I bet you I wouldn't need to be there very long.

That's right. Paul is definitely fed up with domesticity. He's stopped doing the simplest chores. The other day, when it snowed, he didn't even mention the word *shovel*. He got in his car and drove away. He knows I'm afraid to drive in the snow, and I can't back out of our long driveway.

I didn't say anything either. The girls and I cleaned up the whole thing. They weren't happy, but we did it. I'll find some college guys in the neighborhood who can help us next time.

I'm very capable. I've been doing it all for long periods of time, since the year he went to Vietnam. I'm used to it. Of course, it'll be more difficult holding a job too, but it couldn't be worse than going to graduate school full-time as I've done, could it?

You too. I don't even know if you celebrate Christmas. Have a good break then. I'll see you in the new year.

*   *   *

No, not yet, but we did tell the girls. I think that Laura was relieved. She's been under a lot of tension knowing that something was wrong, and that there wasn't anything she could do about it. She's always thought of herself as a miracle worker.

I did. I told them both that it wasn't in any way their fault, and that their father and I will always love them, no matter what. Andrea didn't miss a beat. Immediately she asked if we could get a cat. She knows her dad hates cats.

I said we would, in two weeks, when her father moves out. How's that for blackmail?

Then we told them that we were all going to the mall so they'd know there'll be things the four of us can do together. When we got there, the two of them couldn't ask for stuff fast enough. They are not dumb.

It wasn't bad. I've had worse Christmases. The anniversary was the most difficult day, knowing that we were about to separate. The girls had bought us a lovely glass platter. Talk about feeling guilty. I was really sad for them and for us. Whatever happened to our perfect little family?

That's right, seventeen years. I don't see how I can ever say again that I'm a fast learner.

Supposedly, Paul will have them two weekends each month and during the summer in Maine. We'll take turns with the holidays.

We've been getting some household goods together for Paul: a set of dishes, flatware, sheets, towels, his coffeepots . . . All of a sudden, he remembers which wedding presents came from his side of the family and he wants to take them with him. To make matters worse, his mother has given him a list she made of all the wedding gifts.

Also, the girls have gone with him to see his apartment.

Very little furniture: some lamps, pictures, his damn trunk. His parents are setting him up with some antiques and Oriental rugs. Paul has their Waspy taste.

No, I've never cared for antiques. We have contemporary furniture: white leather, glass, chrome, that sort of thing. Turns out he always hated it. I don't mind an occasional antique, but the entire place—no way.

Each of us has told our own families. It's amazing how little they seem to care, particularly mine. And to think that one of the big reasons we stayed together so long was for them. We wanted—I should get used to saying *I*; I really don't know what Paul wants anymore—I wanted to prove that even though I was so young, I was a responsible person, mature enough to be married, have children, raise a family.

That's right, I turned out to be responsible—and dumb.

When I told my father, he reminded me of an old saying in Spanish: "A enemigo que huye, puente de plata," it's a philosophical version of "good riddance." They never cared for each other those two, my dad and Paul.

I didn't even speak to him. He was away somewhere. I told my sister-in-law. She wasn't surprised in the least, she said, after all the time I've spent alone traveling over there in the summer. It had been a lot more obvious to people than we wanted to admit.

I feel anxious. I'm afraid there is still a shoe waiting to drop. I can't believe it, really. It needs to sink in.

Do I have time to tell you something else?

That's okay, I'll tell you next time. I've already resolved it myself. That's what this therapy is all about, right? Getting me to make the hard decisions without having to check with you first.

I hope so. As completely free as anyone can be with two princesses in tow, a large house, and my first full-time teaching job.

*   *   *

It wasn't easy. It was snowing that morning and blowing hard too. He borrowed a friend's truck, but he did it all himself.

The girls did help him. I went next door and pretended not to look.

That's true. You'd think I would never pretend again, after all the trouble it got me into.

He just said to me, "Ta-ta, I'll see you." He gave the girls a proper good-bye. He hugged them and told them he loved them. I said, "You know where we'll be."

It was sad, but nothing that some of Momma's spaghetti couldn't cure. Andrea looks withdrawn, despite the cat. I alerted their teachers. But in general, they seem to be okay.

Oh yes, we have a cat, Alfred, a spoiled tabby, I'm afraid. He's supposed to sleep in the laundry room, but I keep finding him upstairs when I wake up.

I'm fine. It isn't much different than the last few months—perhaps more work, but less tension. It must be quite a change for Paul, but that's what he wanted. And by the way, there was someone at work.

Yes, a bright young associate he hired about a year ago. I had noticed that she'd blush whenever we ran into her. I don't feel too sorry for him.

I don't either. I'm getting a second chance. I imagine that many people who divorce don't get that. At least now I have an education. The girls are at a good age. It's not like when they were babies. No, I don't feel sorry for myself at all.

Oh, yes. I told you I was going to New York City for the MLA.

The Modern Language Association. I had some job interviews, but I've decided to wait until next year for that since I have my foot in the door for the Bryn Mawr tenure-track position if it comes through. There are enough changes in my life for now.

That's right, and the girls too. I have no intention of moving them or changing their schools.

At the MLA, I ran into all sorts of friends, professors . . . I guess they are colleagues now. I wasn't advertising it, but if they asked me how my family was, I told them I was separated. Period.

You've noticed it already. I have to confess that I took my ring off once before, but that's history now. By the time I saw this professor from Emory on the second day, he already knew. That's how fast news travels in these circles. Anyway, we agreed to have dinner together. Some other people from the convention saw us and sat down with us.

No, I never took a class with him. He taught linguistics and I majored in literature, but I had sort of a crush on him. I knew he was married and had a couple of little kids already.

He's not that much older than me. He just got started earlier.

I am not like my father at all.

No, I'm not being defensive. Let me tell you the rest of the story, okay? We started to meet after the sessions, and then he definitely made a pass at me.

No, this time it wasn't so much that I was flattered. It was that I always liked him. At the university, we used to comment that he wore "Hush Puppies" and laugh. He still does. He's really very handsome. Sort of innocent in a way. Well, not so innocent, really, but I used to think so.

It ended up that I thought about it and told him that I understood why he was propositioning me, that I had always liked him too—still did; but I wasn't ready to get involved or have a tryst or anything. I'm not really sure what he had in mind, since he's still married. And that was that.

Thank you. I'm proud of myself too.

Yes, I have. I've been seeing more of my girlfriends. I have started taking guitar lessons. I have been to a couple of concerts, something Paul and I never did. And I'm making tentative plans for the summer. I've sent a paper to a congress near Madrid.

Not yet. I should find out soon. The organizers know my work, so I think I have a good chance.

I'll keep you posted. I'm sure I'll need to come for a tune-up sooner or later. You have really helped me a lot.

That's not true. Just knowing that I was coming to see you made me focus and center myself.

Yes, free as a bird. Isn't that the American saying? It's been all of four weeks now.

*   *   *

I'm back. It's always going to be like this. He's completely predictable in his unpredictability.

You are close. No, I didn't hear from him on Valentine's Day, but he showed up with a lily plant on Easter, saying that he agreed with me; we needed to work on communicating better if we were ever going to get back together.

I told him he was nuts, that we needed a miracle of biblical proportions to do that. He called me a wiseass, told me to put the lily where "the sun don't shine," and proceeded to leave the house in a huff.

The problem is that he changes his plans at the last minute after we've made arrangements for the girls' weekends. He shows up very early or very late. Some weekends he spoils them with all sorts of shopping; others he's so angry at them that they call me crying, asking me to please pick them up immediately. It's unnerving, to say the least.

They're already getting used to it. Some of their friends are going through the same sort of things. Laura, in particular, has started making her own plans. And that too makes her father upset.

I've tried to be firm, but it isn't easy. It's also very tempting to give in to the girls to make their dad look bad. It's not very conducive for dating.

Yes, I have. Nothing serious. I play tennis with a guy from the theology department at the university. I went to the theater with a photographer from Princeton. I've been out to dinner a couple of times with a guitarist I met through my teacher. He's really smitten with me.

I have no idea how much Paul knows. I'm sure he pumps the girls for information.

I'm glad to hear this is typical. Isn't it ironic that we need to be completely dysfunctional to become a "normal" American family?

You really think we've been dysfunctional for that long?

All right. Here's the story. The latest trick is that I won't be getting child support when the kids are away with their grandparents. I explained to Paul that other than maybe food, I don't save anything when the kids are not home. I still have to pay the mortgage, the utilities. I can't keep a budget according to whatever the kids decide to do.

I know he's desperate, but I need to have a budget I can count on, not depending on the girls' vacations. It's not like I'm getting alimony or anything else. Besides, we agreed.

It isn't official yet. I'm waiting to hear from Bryn Mawr. It looks as if they are going to hire me as an assistant professor, on a tenure-track position! I'm sure I'd enjoy my work there. The students are wonderful; they're mostly women except for an occasional guy from Haverford College. Perfect for a "flaming feminist," as Paul's been calling me.

I have tried talking to his parents. That was one of the first things I did. My mother-out-law . . .

That's what I call them now, my out-laws. I knew they never cared for me. Anyway, she said, "Inmaculada, dear, that's between you and Paul." End of story. I haven't spoken to them again.

Of course, I don't want to say, "Then they are not going," because I'd be punishing the girls. If I had to count on their father, I wouldn't have any time to myself. It's all very unfair.

Right now I have plans to give a paper in Spain in July. I'm getting ready to buy my ticket. Paul probably thinks I'm meeting someone there.

I am not seeing François. I never heard from him again. And Gus, remember him? He writes only every so often, but that's all. We've stayed in touch. It was a matter of principle, and I like that.

I think you are right, what I really need is a good attorney. I never knew I could be fired by my therapist.

No, it's not a bad sign at all. I'll make one more appointment then.

*   *   *

I knew the last weeks before I left would be difficult. Paul manages to come up with some new threat each step of the way. I pretend to be immune to it, but inside I still worry. He's losing clout, even if he still has control of the purse strings.

There is no way he could keep the girls from me. They wouldn't allow it, and he knows it. Sometimes I even feel sorry for him. He can be so pathetic. Like last week, when he said he's only happy when he's with Vietnam vets. So where does that leave the rest of us mortals? He still has problems with the war that he hasn't resolved in over fifteen years.

I can't help him with that anymore. We were so young then, and we had absolutely no help with all the adjustments. It's amazing we survived as well as we did.

I'm doing all right. It isn't easy, but surprisingly, I'm happier than I've been in a long time. I'm so glad my job situation worked out. I don't know if this'll be the place for me for my entire career, but it's a solid start. Laura could get an excellent education at Bryn Mawr, and she seems agreeable to applying there. I can't believe she'll be doing that next year already.

And Andrea will be starting high school in one more year. If only Paul and I would stop arguing and making things worse. They appear to have adjusted well to our separation. They even like Sarah.

Paul's girlfriend. I think I've told you about her. They work together. Both girls say they prefer it when she's around because their father is nicer to them. They seem more protective when it comes to my dating.

Andrea gave me a hard time when I brought Ewen home.

He's the guitarist. It's a family name. I thought I had mentioned him to you.

Yes, he's nuts about me. He even understands that I'd want to go out with other people. He's been divorced for several years and has had a chance "to see what's out there," as he puts it. He's not eager to date around.

He's very confident. He's willing to wait. He wanted to come with me to Spain, but I asked him not to. He studied there, speaks Spanish quite well. He's also very playful and lots of fun.

Anyway, Andrea announced a few minutes before he arrived, after we had discussed it and she agreed to be civil to him, that she wouldn't come down from her room to say hi. I had to think fast. I told her that if she did so, I would stay in my room the next time she had friends over, instead of making snacks for them or agreeing to drive them anywhere.

Laura was a big help. She told her sister that I would do it too, and then she'd be sorry.

When Ewen arrived, Andrea was still upstairs. We visited for a few minutes, and soon we heard little steps coming down. Andrea showed up with her favorite book, *Where the Sidewalk Ends*, and asked Ewen to read it to her.

Now they are competing with their Spanish vocabulary. It's not quite *Brady Bunch* material, but we are having fun.

The truth? He knows more words, but her accent is better. He needs to work on his Castilian pronunciation if he wants to get into my heart.

I guess so. But I know it's too soon. For one thing, I'm still married.

No, he doesn't. He was only married a short time. But he loves his nieces and nephews, and he's the godfather of his best friend's daughter. He sure seems to get along with mine. I understand it's too soon for this as well.

Yes, he's gotten into my bed too. So far so good. That's all I want to say. It brings back bad memories if I start talking to anyone about my sex life.

No, they haven't met yet. I have been nothing short of charming with Sarah, though.

The attorney was helpful. Basically, he used Paul's agreement as a model and made it official. Paul was having a good day, I guess, and he signed it without any problems. It's a good thing I have a job because I've received two bills from the attorney's office already.

As far as I know, he'll represent me. Paul has a big shot from Camden, as if we had millions to share.

That's good, I can only afford one of you at the same time.

That's right, just for a short stay this summer. I'm giving a paper and buying books—that's all. I'd like to bring the girls with me next year and have some family vacation time then.

After the congress, I'll spend some time in Cape Cod with Ewen and some of his friends. He rents a big old place every year and gives guitar master classes there. An odd assortment of people join him. They take turns cooking . . .

Yes, but don't tell my out-laws. Sort of grown-up hippies, the *Return of the Secaucus Seven* type. Now did you see that film?

I have no idea how I'll fit in. I hope the girls will be able to join us there too. Maybe I'll pick them up in Maine. It's a few hours' drive.

We'll see. Something completely new, that's for sure. You have a great summer too!

*   *   *

IV

Summer 1982

Viernes, 9 de julio

What's with me and airports? It seems that I'm always starting and ending things when I travel. Maybe that's the cross immigrants bear—this coming and going, missing something, no matter where we are. I have to confess that I don't feel like leaving at all this time. That was such a tender good-bye from Ewen. I almost wished I had made plans to leave with him, but he didn't try to pressure me into it. He said he understood and respected my decision. What a contrast with last night's departure. I could tell the girls were sad. Not because we've been having such a congenial time together, but because they dread being with their dad. There he was, sitting in the driveway, not even bothering to come in the house to pick them up and say hi or bye to me. It's only a week, and then their grandparents will pick them up to go to Maine, where they do have fun and get to see their old dog, Willie, again. I need to come up with a different plan for next summer.

So much for going incognito, though. I shouldn't be surprised that there are several academics on the flight, just days before this big congress. It's good that we are not sitting together because I want to reread my paper to make sure that it's the right length of time. But I'm glad I've made arrangements with them to take the bus from Madrid to the town of Pastrana, where the congress is being held. It sounds interesting, but it is definitely isolated. At least I know I'll be part of this group. The closer I get to giving my paper, the more doubts I have about it. After being so excited about his novel, now I'm not even sure that F. Santos is such a seminal writer.

Ewen and I have been getting along well despite our differences. Last week I had taken care of my entire house, packed the girls' luggage and my own, attended to a hundred little details, but his one-bedroom place was still a mess and his car needed to be tuned. I'm glad I spoke up and said I was exhausted, so I took a nap while he finished getting ready for his trip to Cape Cod. The best part was waking up to find him there next to me. I like it that he's strong but tender at the same time. He's always ready to make love without any props, and if I just suggest that I'm not up for it (not so often, it's true) or I don't like something, he's patient and very considerate. I had to get used to his mild temper. I have never been with someone like him.

In some ways, his family is even more ethnic than mine. They are not religious either, but they follow cultural Jewish traditions like foods, especially during the holidays. Ewen seems close to them—a good sign, particularly to his sister and his mother, who's every bit as eccentric as my dad. For them I am a *shiksa*, a gentile woman (to make matters worse

I heard "chicksa" at first). I am not the first one, though, since both brothers have married outside their faith. Years ago, it would have been a scandal to date someone like him in Spain, but since Franco died, all the religions are not only allowed but it's also trendy for people to speak openly of their cultural roots. It's almost funny; Santa Teresa, Cervantes, Franco himself—all have a newly discovered Jewish heritage. Maybe I should have brought my own pet Jew along with me.

Domingo, 11 de julio

What a pleasure being alone! Here I am, eating by myself at the hotel. It's not a big place, but it's friendly and very well situated in an area of Madrid I am familiar with, the Barrio de Salamanca. Here I thought I was jet-lagged all these years, and it turns out it was my family that was making me dizzy. I took a long nap when I first arrived, then showered, watched the news, and by the time I was out in the street, I felt as refreshed as if I hadn't traveled at all. The newer superstore chains, like Crisol and VIPS, even El Corte Inglés, don't close in the afternoon anymore, so I can eat anytime and get the shopping done whenever I want to. I'll leave the heavier books in the hotel since I'll be back here one more day after the congress.

I called my brother last evening just to say hi and let him know that I was in Madrid but wouldn't have a chance to visit them. This time I'm here for professional reasons, but next summer, I want to bring the girls so the cousins can get to know one another better. I have to admit that Junior sounded as relieved as I was. His mother-in-law is in poor health, and they've been running around between the mountains and the city nonstop. My sister-in-law got on the phone and asked me, whispering, if I was going to see Agustín. How could I explain to her that I no longer need to come here to see anyone? I am separated, and I can see whomever I want anywhere I want. She seemed so disappointed with my new status. "Separated? Why not divorced already?" she wanted to know. She couldn't believe that divorce takes so long in the States. I have to get used to the New Spain myself. It seems that the newer the laws, the more progressive they are. Just when I thought I was a trendsetter, I'm behind the eight ball again.

This morning I took a long walk and ended up in front of my old school. Madrid was deserted at that time of day, and the streets were cool and shiny from the early-morning dew. Even on Sundays, the gardens had been watered and the fresh smell of wet dirt permeated the air. El General Mola boulevard is called Príncipe de Vergara now since all the streets have been renamed back to their original names from before the Spanish Civil War. The main gate was open. Maybe they say mass for the neighborhood parishioners now, although that was a sore point when I was a student because they didn't use to. I went in to take a look. The buildings seemed to have shrunk, but the trees were a lot larger than I remembered them, with huge shadows over the walks and benches surrounding the gardens. The shrubs and the rosebushes, trimmed and shaped to perfection, could be the very same that were there years ago when I was a schoolgirl. The small statute of the Virgin Mary at the end, in one corner, still has her arms open and the palms facing up, welcoming the flowers we used to give her in the month of May or an occasional bouquet brought by a former student transformed into a new bride.

As I was walking back around the cloister side of the main building, a nun came out at the top of the double staircase. When she heard that I had attended school there, the nun invited me to enter and visit. I almost said no without thinking that I wasn't in any particular hurry. All of a sudden, I was sliding down the same shiny, cold long dark hallways of my school. The few classrooms that were open looked exactly the same as they were over twenty years ago: the small desks arranged by height, the large windows, a thick pad of closed maps hanging in the opposite wall. The blackboard in front, perfectly clean now, is not full of kings' names according to dynasties or, worse yet, fractions or square roots. I was speechless, full of emotion, as if I were that little girl who walked those halls, first in a line of many little girls just like me—always the first with my last name, *Abello*. The nun asked me who had been my teachers: *Madre* Eulalia, so big and scary; *Madre* María Margarita, who knew my dad from Valencia and made sure I had a scholarship; *Madre* Encarnación, a real *hueso*, a tough cookie, who taught math; and my favorite, *Madre* Matilde, the sewing teacher. No, she didn't know any of them. That's one thing about nuns: one never knows their age. Maybe this one was younger than I thought at first.

The door that joins the cloister with the school was open. I had never seen it this way before, and I looked in with the same curiosity I must have felt as a student when the nuns disappeared through it, sliding—seemingly footless—as if they were skating on ice. We stopped to see the class pictures in the Salón de Actos, the Great Hall, and there, with identical gray uniforms, white shirts, and red bow ties, I was repeated in several frames. My hair was dark and shiny in braids of different lengths, also with red bows; my legs looked thin in their black stockings and chunky shoes. I had black bows in one of the pictures; it must have been the year we were in mourning for my maternal grandfather. My companion nun brought me back to reality when she commented how tall I am now, when I looked so thin and small in the school pictures. She's not the first person to notice this. That's another miracle of us immigrants; we become different, altogether new persons when we leave our countries.

This entire Sunday has been enveloped in nostalgia after the visit to my old school. I have started to think, as I write in this journal, that what I would really like to do is write my memoirs: my life in Valencia, where I was born, when it was a sad city still recovering from the Civil War under the brilliant Mediterranean sky, my family's move to Madrid, so big and new then, but so strangely familiar now. I realize that I'll need to do research to get ahead in my field and earn tenure in the American academic system, but who says I can't write something creative as well? My area of specialization is from the years of Franco's regime to the present anyway; it could be another way in which my personal and professional life meet. I can't wait to tell Ewen about it. Although I've stopped my guitar lessons, hearing him making music these past few months has made my creative juices flow. His playing is somewhat like his lovemaking—gentle but assured and precise. He hardly ever plays a wrong note.

Martes, 13 de julio

So much for progressive Spain. It really is like the travel brochure—a land of contrasts. Less than two hours from Madrid, one steps out of the bus into the main square of Pastrana. A Renaissance jewel, Pastrana is just about the quaintest little town I've ever visited. Doña Ana de Mendoza y de la Cerda was Pastrana's most famous citizen. She was Duchess of Pastrana and Princess of Éboli. This Renaissance lady and patroness of the arts married when she was twelve years old to the much-older Ruy Gómez da Silva, the king's secretary and best friend. She was a supporter of Santa Teresa's reformation of the Carmelite order until they had a falling out, when her husband died. After his death, she spent three years in a convent with her ladies-in-waiting and all the court's luxuries, as was the custom in those days, but returned to public life, forming an alliance with the king's undersecretary of state. They were accused of betraying state secrets, which led to her arrest. Doña Ana de Mendoza was kept captive in the tower of Pastrana's ducal Palace from 1581 until she died in1592. She was allowed to see the light for only one hour each day, thus the square is named La Plaza de la Hora.

A walk through Pastrana's small streets, which open like a fan from the square, will take you by the gothic Colegiata, where the princess is buried with her husband. It is the site of an old synagogue standing next to the Inquisition House and the famous fountain of the four spigots, *de los cuatro caños,* where the children and the goats drink at the same time. Everywhere you look, there are houses with coats of arms or crosses of the knights of Calatrava on their beveled arches. The heavy wooden doors are often finished with square nails, whimsical door knockers, or elaborate iron locks that remain from centuries of handcrafted work. It's easy to get lost in Pastrana's old history and forget the fast pace of the New Spain.

I'm staying in an old Franciscan convent from the sixteenth century, which has been turned into a conference center. From the outside, it looks imposing, made from huge boulders the exact same color of the rocky hills around here. The inside is finished all in white, and it's cool despite the relentless daytime heat. The old architectural details—exposed beams, iron bars, window shutters—create a completely modern effect. All the furnishings are rustic but comfortable. In an interior patio, there is a pool surrounded by grape arbors and all kinds of fruit trees: fig, cherry, lemon. The chaise lounges hide in the shade, and it's amazingly quiet despite the fact that the convent is at full capacity. The conference rooms are at ground level, and people meander in and out of the stone arches that connect them to the central patio where evening receptions are held. It has five beautiful fountains with sleepy water flowing where the birds bathe in the morning and in the late-afternoon sun. My favorite spot is a smaller patio, ideal for meditation and solitude, with an herb garden and a few benches. Each area has a marker with the name of the plant and its magical uses: *valeriana* for sleeping, *lavanda* for perfume, *basílico* for cooking (especially tomatoes and vegetables), *camomila* for teas and to soothe an upset stomach, *cilantro, menta, romero, tomillo* . . . Given its intimate size, it's shady most of the day, and butterflies flitter softly over the gentle flowers as the wind stirs the scented air capriciously.

Jueves, 15 de julio

I think that my paper was well received, better than I expected. Since there isn't that much to do around here, the *congresistas* are quite responsible about attending the sessions regularly. We also eat most of our meals together in what probably was the monks' old refectory, which opens into yet another patio covered or partially open with big white retractable awnings, depending on the weather and the time of day. The food itself is an adventure. Today for the two o'clock meal (some things haven't changed at all; they still eat very late in Spain), we had a sampler of local foods. For the first course, white asparagus with homemade *allioli* or mayonnaise (so far, so good); for the main course (and here is where I got in trouble), rabbit stew with olives, rosemary, and thyme, and *migas* on the side. *Migas* is a traditional dish of the region, made with leftover bread sautéed with vegetables. My mother used to make her own version during the years we still lived in Valencia when no one could afford to waste any food. As for the rabbit, there were conflicting opinions. Some of the people started saying they had actually heard the shots from the hunters very early in the morning; others swore that the rabbit tasted just like chicken. I can't attest to the first since I've been sleeping very soundly lately, but the second is definitely not true. I got away without tasting it all the years my family lived in Spain, but here I was caught having to eat the poor animal. Thank goodness for the *berros* (watercress) and *puerros* (leeks) salad, which may sound like a tongue twister in Spanish but was delicious; besides, I had practically seen the salad grow in the herb garden. Fresh cherries and figs were served before we finished our feast with local sweets: *bizcochos borrachos* (literally, drunken cake) and *yemas de Santa Teresa* (I won't even try to translate it). The wines were also from the region, and judging from the long naps people took under the trees, they must have been quite tasty as well.

Sábado, 17 de julio

I left the congress early on Friday to meet my father's publisher. Well, now he's my publisher also—what the hell! I can't believe I've signed a contract to publish my dissertation. I'm sure having a known last name didn't hurt, but he did say that the deciding factor was the work itself. I mentioned to him the idea of writing a book of memoirs, and he seemed amenable to it, particularly because my father won't be writing them at this point. Now that's a concept I hadn't thought about: to write the book he wouldn't write. I answered something flippant like this book would be my story and my dad's role would be only that of one more player, not the protagonist. Then there is the issue of language. To make a real break, I'd want to start publishing in the States, but I haven't written much in English, and I don't know if I could be as clever or play with the language the way I can in Spanish. I need to think a lot more about this whole thing. Maybe research wouldn't be such a problem after all. I definitely would want to work on a woman writer next time. Carmen Martín Gaite or one of the more contemporary ones, like Rosa Montero, seem very appealing to me.

The publisher and I met at Casa Mingo, a typical restaurant next to San Antonio de la Florida, the church with Goya's frescoes, one of the best-kept secrets of Madrid. In Casa Mingo, they serve only roasted chicken, fries, and cider from Asturias. I always have to remember that cider in this country has alcohol in it. Maybe it isn't much, but enough to make me tipsy, which was about the last thing I wanted just then. It's a family place, full of children running around and making much too much noise, as Spanish kids are known to do. Ewen would love to be in this old part of the city. He is such a Spaniard wannabe, but I know that there is an entire other Spain that he hasn't seen, and I would love to show it to him. I bought him a *boina*, a beret, to substitute for that Borsalino hat he always wears. Of course, now he calls it his lucky charm since he had worn it on the night we met.

I've thought a lot about him. I'm eager to be with him again, chatting nonstop about art and films, which we both love. I can see that we are becoming committed to each other. Not that we have plans to move in together, but certainly to have an exclusive relationship. So much for the "dating around" that I've said, only half in jest, I've always wanted to do. It's too soon and too late at the same time. Too soon for someone like Ewen in my life and too late to see other people since I've already met him and I'm falling in love.

I've come to the conclusion that Spain is great for a short visit like this one. I think that I've overdosed before and that's why, by the time I leave, I swear never to come back. Now I am making mental plans to come back, not only with Ewen, but also with the girls.

I have this rake sitting next to me who doubts that my boyfriend is going to show up to drive me all the way from JFK to Cape Cod. Yet I'm so sure that I hadn't even thought what a long distance it was. I wish I had my needlepoint with me to keep him quiet. I've noticed that men won't talk to women who are knitting or doing something domestic like that in public. Better still, I'm going to take a nap and dream about being in Ewen's arms.

Lunes, 19 de julio

I see today's date and wonder if there were demonstrations in Spain yesterday like last year. There is no TV here, but I doubt it would make the news in the States anyway.

Cape Cod reminds me somewhat of Maine. Less rain and fewer rocks, but the same cool breezes, pine trees, and crisp ocean water. I'm writing alone (a small miracle here) on the deck next to the dining room. I can hear the students practicing their scales on the guitar. Ewen is practicing too in our room, but he's on the other side of this huge place and I don't hear his usual repertoire. Greg and Jeffrey, the two actors, left early this morning for a drive to Martha's Vineyard. Lori, one of Ewen's old girlfriends, is out with her new flame, a chick from Nantucket! The couple from the Baltimore orchestra is shopping because it's their turn to cook tonight. I'm not sure what they are making, but that's one of the charms of this place. Everyone gets to share their specialties without getting tired of cooking all the time.

I said I would make a paella after the girls arrive. Their grandparents are bringing them on Thursday, and I'm tickled pink about it (and a bit anxious, I have to confess). Turns out that my out-laws don't mind dropping them off on their way to Boston to meet some old friends. I have a feeling they didn't want to entertain Paul and Sarah, who'll be arriving in Maine soon. My, they are not going to be pleased with this setup here either. The girls sounded so excited about having a room by the students' quarters that they didn't complain about having to share it. And when they heard that a raccoon has taken over the front porch, Laura assured me they know how to get rid of him. We'll see.

Ewen's specialty is hugs. He gave me the sweetest, longest, tightest hug in the world when I finally came out of Customs in JFK. Neither one of us said a word for a short time, just held on to each other, breathing rhythmically. Ewen says that he's not asking me the next time, he's just coming along. Despite the traffic and the heat, we had a pleasant drive all the way up here. It didn't seem long at all, and I felt completely awake. It was dark when we arrived, and we ate some leftovers in the kitchen. Some of the students and other friends stopped by to say hi. I could tell that Ewen had been talking about me. They all seemed very curious and relaxed. It's part of the culture here to be friendly and social.

Our bedroom is very attractive. It has two dormer windows with a view of the water, and it's shaded by the tall pines. There is no air conditioner, but most of the time, there is an ocean breeze and the ceiling fan is a big help. The best part is that we have our own bathroom, so we can have some more privacy. In fact, we made love in the shower as soon as we went upstairs. He surprised me coming in after me without asking. We lathered each other, and as he was rinsing my back, I could feel him entering me ever so slippery. When I woke up yesterday, my thick hair was still wet and we were hugging each other like *dos cucharitas* (two teaspoons). We made love again, quietly this time, so as to not wake up the people downstairs.

On Sundays, people sleep in or sit around in their pajamas reading the *New York Times* and the *Boston Globe*. Everyone helps themselves to breakfast or lunch. The only meal we have together is dinner. The living room and a front parlor are full of books, games, and magazines. The screened-in porch has a Ping-Pong table and comfortable wicker furniture. Several students have brought their wives or girlfriends; two of them are pregnant, and we all fuss over them. Another is writing her dissertation, and I have given her all kinds of pointers as if I were an expert (and to think that it has been less than a year since I defended mine!). There are small groups who usually do things together; Bob, the retired music professor, goes out with "the boys" while the students hang around the house—I don't think they have as much money to spend. Ewen is expecting Michael, a close friend of his, who is coming with his two children, a boy and a girl several years younger than Laura and Andrea. Greg and Jeffrey are preparing an impromptu performance, a "happening," for the following weekend. We'll know our roles only a few minutes before. There are no rehearsals.

I'm very taken by this relaxed lifestyle. It's all so different from anything I've ever experienced before, or is it that my love for Ewen colors all my sensations now? As soon as he finished practicing, we are off to the beach. There are no classes on Sundays.

Viernes, 23 de julio

Yesterday was such an emotional day! I felt so nervous anticipating the girls' arrival. In a way, it worked out well that it was Ewen's turn to cook and we were busy getting ready for that. He made a mighty tasty bouillabaisse—good thing I bought some saffron in Spain. We went shopping for the seafood first thing in the morning, and it took until noon just to get the fish stock prepared. I set the table and cleaned the girls' room. It's across the hall from Michael's children, who are also sharing a room. I bought them some Indian bedspreads in Provincetown to dress it up a bit. The presents from Spain were on the bureau waiting for them. Their bathroom is at the end of the hall, and that makes them feel grown-up since some of the students also use it. The two of them looked so lovely when they got out of the car, tanned and healthy too. Laura always has such a mature demeanor when she comes back from visiting her grandparents. I can tell she's been helping take care of her sister. Andrea just ran over and gave me a big hug (I can never get too many of those). Both of them seemed content to see Ewen again. He showed them where their room was and gave them a quick tour of the place. Soon they were carrying their bags and making themselves at home. The ones who were very uncomfortable were my out-laws. They refused to stay for dinner, although it was almost time to eat, and since Ewen had cooked, it seemed natural to invite them. I never thought I could feel sorry for them, but this time I did. They were out of place and old-fashioned—stiff, really. By the time they were ready to leave, Laura and Andrea had disappeared, so we had to hunt them down to say good-bye to their grandparents and properly thank them. I could see that Constance was about to start crying, and Paul Senior shook my hand as if I were a business acquaintance.

I had decided to speak to both girls separately right after dinner and let them know that Ewen and I were in a serious relationship. Talk about uncomfortable. Laura acted as if I were insulting her. "Please, Mom. We already know," she said condescendingly. Andrea, on the other hand, had a million questions: "Is he moving in with us?" "Will he take care of the lawn?" "He isn't allergic to cats, is he?" "Can I take guitar lessons with him?" No on all counts, I told her, but maybe he would teach her some music. "That's okay," she said. "I still like him." She's always been the practical one in the family. I'm sure she won't have so much trouble deciding who is a good man for her when she grows up.

Now I practically have to make an appointment to see the girls during the day. The two of them have already asked me if we can come back next year. How's that for loyalty?

Domingo, 25 de julio

I haven't had as much time to write as before, but I've been thinking a lot about my future. I'm going to try writing fiction instead of memoirs. That way, I not only get to relive my past but I can also recreate it the way I wish it had been or the way it could have been. No one but I will know what's fiction and what's not. I would have more freedom to change characters and point of view too. It would be like an experiment, mixing this and that, and not knowing how it'll turn out until the end. I may be wrong, but one needs to be famous or old to write a memoir, and I'm neither. To write a novel, I just need to be gutsy, right? I haven't decided on the language question yet. Perhaps I would use either Spanish or English depending on the character or the situation. Now my parents, or my brother for that matter, speaking in English would really be fictitious.

It seems that we have been doing everything with Michael and his children. It turns out they are going through a divorce as well. I feel sorry for the kids; they seem so innocent and lonely. Now why don't I feel sorry for my own children? I guess I have confidence that they are going to be all right. And I truly believe that Paul is not that connected to his daughters while Michael is such a great father. The girls tell me that now Paul is looking into moving to Southern California, where it's warm. Couldn't he go any farther? What is he, a bird who needs to migrate to warmer climates? What about seeing the girls? When I mentioned it to Ewen, he said not to worry, that it would mean more time for us with them. How can I tell him that worries me too?

This evening is the students' concert. I can hear them practicing big time today. They are so endearing. They all act like mini Ewens, with their trimmed nails, same mannerisms, and same care with their instruments. A couple of them even look like him, with long hair and beards. They weren't so cute last night, though, when I heard them cavorting in the water close to midnight. I wanted to go out and see if Laura was there with them, but Ewen wouldn't hear of it. Didn't I go skinny-dipping when I was their age? I don't think so. I got married young, but everything else I did rather late. Andrea claimed this morning that she slept through the whole thing, and Laura said that she didn't go in the water because it was too cold. That wasn't the point, I said. Was she dressed? She's growing up so much lately. Soon she'll be talking about the junior prom, then senior year . . . I don't know if I'm ready.

Martes, 27 de julio

It's been a lot quieter here since several of the students left. Other people have arrived, and there are a couple more teenagers with their parents. The girls seem to be having such a great time. And frankly, I am too. I can't remember relaxing for so many days in a row. Ewen has started a Ping-Pong competition, and there are all kinds of elaborate schedules posted in the porch. Laura is determined to win the whole thing, but I've warned her that Ewen is pretty determined when he gets an idea in his head. Yesterday we went to visit Truro and the sand dunes. We took this long walk by the cranberry bogs. I turned around at one point, and Ewen was coming behind me holding Andrea's hand. I can't explain why, but I felt so emotional at that moment, I almost started crying. Afterward, we stopped in some of the ceramic studios and watched the artisans making their wares. The girls and Ewen want to go sailing, but I'm not crazy about the idea. They are waiting for the right weather, breezy and not too hot.

Tomorrow is my turn to cook. I'm going to make a fish paella. This is the perfect spot for it. My mother used to make it when we lived in Spain, before she started putting chicken and pork in it because she couldn't find the fresh fish she liked in the American Midwest. I remember her saying that you just go to the market and buy whatever fish looks good for the stock, then use squid for flavor, shrimps and mussels for the topping. Now "What is a good-looking fish?" Andrea asked me. I told her that one needs to have the Spanish gene to be able to tell, so she will when she gets older. That opened a can of worms because Ewen told them that he also has a Spanish gene somewhere, which is why he loves the classical guitar so much. "But he doesn't cook paella," Andrea observed with her ten-year-old logic. Now that she is into gene theory, she is also sure that the paella gene must be recessive because Laura can only cook macaroni and cheese.

Ewen and I make love almost every day. Nap time is my favorite, like today. It makes me feel a bit naughty. People were running around, and we could hear their voices and occasional laughter. The air was warm, and it smelled of pine trees and ocean water. We started teasing each other as we often do; he loves to make me laugh. I told him that his skin felt damp, that it must be because of all the years of practice he's had at being a lounge lizard. Mine was dry and hot to the touch, like freshly baked bread, because I had been reading in the sun. We became quiet when we got down to business. He put his hand through my thick hair and pulled it gently away from my face while I looked into his hazel eyes and told him that I loved him. My eyes were closed by the time he came, but I'm familiar already with his earnest expression and the tight muscles in his chest. He wasn't ready to sleep yet, though. He needed to take care of "the little lady," as he says, and he wanted to know where I get my horny gene from.

Viernes, 30 de julio

I'm up before anyone else. They are all worn-out from the fun and games. One of the new teenagers won at Ping-Pong, so Ewen is looking for a new venue; he's teaching us to play casino, a card game, but I won't be surprised if he changes his mind because, so far, I've won the first three games. Beginner's luck, I know. It's raining this morning and it's quite chilly. I'm sitting inside looking out of the front windows, but it was sunny and crispy all day yesterday. They finally went sailing in the afternoon. I rode with them to the rental place to take some pictures. A nice woman offered to take ours so "the whole family" could be in it, and we all agreed without any explanations. There we were, the four of us, except that one-fourth is different. Maybe we are all different now in this new configuration.

Ewen took the girls sailing, and I had to go down the road to a nearby beach to wait for them since our place is all rocks and doesn't really have a beach to speak of. I waited for what seemed like a long time before I could see their catamaran coming around a bend, leaning on one side. Maybe it was windier than I thought out in the open sea. I could make out Ewen and the girls hanging together on the starboard side. I went to the water's edge and started to wave at them profusely. It was funny since the one thing they couldn't do was wave back; they had their hands full as it was. Before I knew it, they were close enough that I could see their faces. The three of them, with matching orange vests on, wearing three identical smiles as well.

This vacation is coming to an end, but I don't have to say good-bye to anyone or hide anything. It is different from other years. I don't know where Ewen and I will end up, but for now we are fine the way things are. I keep thinking about ideas for my fictional autobiography or whatever genre it's going to be. I am wondering why I didn't keep a journal while Paul was in Vietnam. What really happened to him and to me during that time so long ago? Maybe now is the time for me to finally write about that year, which I have never done before.

Tonight is the happening, and we leave for Philadelphia on Sunday. I hear dishes clattering in the kitchen; someone else is finally up.

Sábado, 31 de julio

After sleeping so well for weeks, I'm awake in the middle of the night, and I can't get to sleep. Ewen snores, although he'll deny it in the morning. He says none of his lady friends has ever accused him of that before. Can I help it if they were all zombies? I keep playing the happening in my head. It was just amazing. Jeffrey and Greg gave each of us a piece of paper with simple instructions: what to do, when to do it, and what to wear. We weren't supposed to share our information with anyone else. Everyone received their script at different, unexpected times. I was in the downstairs bathroom when I saw a slip of paper under the door with my name on it. "Read any paragraph out loud from your Camus book, each time after Bob and Michael finish speaking. Wear jeans and a t-shirt." I figured out that Ewen was going to play the guitar because I heard him practice a couple of new pieces, which he had stopped doing the last few days. I had no idea of anyone else's role, other than Bob and Michael talking to each other. The girls were taking it all very seriously, and I didn't even try asking them about their roles for fear they'd tell on me.

After dinner, the doors to the living room were closed, and we could hear Jeffrey and Greg rearranging the furniture. The rest of us waited quietly outside, smiling nervously, until they opened the doors and, in silence, took turns walking each of us in, as if they were ushers at a wedding. Once we were all in our assigned spaces, they gave Ewen a nod, and he started playing his guitar, which he did for the entire time of the performance, beginning with a *milonga*, one of my favorite pieces. The smallest children were busy arranging their GI Joes, making warlike noises every few minutes, shooting one another's soldiers down. Michael's daughter reads the obituaries from the *Boston Globe* in a shrill voice. The couple from Baltimore went in and out of the kitchen, offering drinks and meringues. Laura reads aloud the wedding announcements from the Sunday *New York Times*.

The other teenagers danced behind the sofas, frequently changing partners. Andrea went around asking questions to everyone: "Why? How come? What does that mean?" Greg and Jeffrey would run in and out of the porch area and play a few minutes of Ping-Pong, moving their limbs and faces without uttering a sound. Other people laughed out loud unexpectedly. My own voice reading the Spanish translation of a French author was no more absurd than anyone else's actions. We had a pretty good idea but, at the same time, didn't know what everyone else would do. We suspected, but weren't sure, when the happening would end. And when it did, we all stood up and broke into a loud applause, moved to tears by the mystery of life mirrored by an impromptu summer performance.

Acknowledgements

For me writing is not a solitary occupation, particularly since this is my first novel written completely in English. Thus, I have worked with several writers' groups in Philadelphia that have read and commented on my work. It started with the Big Jar Writers' Group and the Rittenhouse Writers' Group, led by James Rahn, and workshops by Janet Benton, Susan Perloff and Marc Schuster; my thanks to them and all the participants, for their support and insight. There were some early readers of the manuscript who offered constructive criticism: Carlos Rojas, who has encouraged me more than he knows and Bernard F. Stehle, who also took my picture for this book; thank you both. I also want to thank my editor, Tamar Tulin, who so carefully edited my entire manuscript and was readily available for consultation. I sincerely appreciate the materials that John S. Day Jr. lent me about Vietnam, including his mother's albums, which I didn't even know existed. My heartfelt appreciation goes to Dwayne Booth, also known as the political cartoonist Mr. Fish, for his wondrous illustrations of the three novellas; from the moment I saw them I feared they would be the best part of my book.

This novel is dedicated to the memory of my late husband Peter Ewen Segal, who died of cancer in 2006, after more than twenty years of marriage and before he had a chance to read this book. I believe that he would have liked the character he inspired.

Made in the USA
Lexington, KY
05 August 2011